Switched!

TJ and the TIME STUMBLERS

BOOK 5
Switched!

Bill Myers

Tyndale House Publishers, Inc.
Carol Stream, Illinois

Visit Tyndale's website for kids at www.tyndale.com/kids.

Visit Bill Myers's website at www.billmyers.com.

TYNDALE and Tyndale's quill logo are registered trademarks of Tyndale House Publishers, Inc.

Switched!

Designed by Stephen Vosloo

Edited by Sarah Mason

Published in association with the literary agency of Alive Communications, Inc., 7680 Goddard Street, Suite 200, Colorado Springs, CO 80920, www.alivecommunications.com.

For manufacturing information regarding this product, please call 1-800-323-9400.

Library of Congress Cataloging-in-Publication Data

Myers, Bill, date.
  Switched! / Bill Myers.
    p. cm. — (TJ and the time stumblers ; bk. 5)
    Summary: Twenty-third-century time travelers Tuna and Herby's fumbled attempt to repair their futuristic gadgets land TJ, the only person who can see them, in the body of her nemesis, television star Hester Breakahart.
    ISBN 978-1-4143-3457-8 (sc)
  [1. Conduct of life—Fiction.   2. Identity—Fiction.   3. Junior high schools—Fiction.
  4. Schools—Fiction.   5. Time travel—Fiction.   6. Family life—California—Fiction.
  7. Malibu (Calif.)—Fiction.]   I. Title.
  PZ7.M98234Swi 2012
  [Fic]—dc23   2011031338

Printed in the United States of America

18   17   16   15   14   13   12
7   6   5   4   3   2   1

For Jenny.
Thanks for your love these many years.
Our family will miss you.

CHAPTER ONE

Beginnings . . .

TIME TRAVEL LOG:

Malibu, California, January 23

Begin Transmission:

Bruce Bruiseabone is closing in. Must find fuel for time-travel pod and begin journey home. No doubt subject will be brokenhearted. Someday, as hard as it'll be, she may get over me.

End Transmission

Chad Steel did his best to smile as the New Kid did her best to sing. He might have succeeded if her screeching didn't make his face cringe and his eyes water. And don't even ask about the dogs across the street. The poor things were howling like they were being tortured. Honestly, you'd think the Humane Society would force the school to close their choir room windows.

It's not that the New Kid was bad . . .

She was TERRIBLE!

(Sorry, I didn't mean to yell, but it's the only way you could hear me over all her shrieking and screaming and, of course, Mr. Hatemijob's sobbing.) Malibu Junior High's cranky choir director had asked the New Kid to try out for a solo in their spring concert. She was pretty shy and reluctant about it, but Mr. Hatemijob kept insisting she try. So finally she agreed. It would have been better for everyone (including Mr. Hatemijob's breakfast) if she hadn't.

Once his ears stopped ringing (and his stomach stopped heaving), Mr. Hatemijob smiled at the New Kid and said the most encouraging words he could find. "Well, now, your singing is so . . . how can I put it? . . . the worst thing I've ever heard in my entire life!"

And since he was a teacher, he also felt he should give a little instruction.

"Maybe you should transfer from my class and attend another that would put your unique vocal skills to better use."

"Yeah—" Hesper Breakahart giggled from across the choir room—"like sign language."

And since Hesper giggled, all the Hesper wannabes giggled. (When you star in your own TV series on the Dizzy Channel, you have lots of wannabes giggling whenever you giggle.)

But Chad could see how the New Kid's cheeks burned with embarrassment. And even though he and Hesper were a couple (at least according to Hesper), he heard himself say, "Come on, guys, she wasn't *that* bad."

Of course everyone looked at him like he was nuts. Well, everyone but Hesper Breakahart. It's hard to look at someone like he's nuts when you're busy shooting death rays at him from your eyeballs. *No one* disagreed with Hesper Breakahart.

But Chad kinda liked the New Kid. It wasn't just because they were next-door neighbors. It was because there was something kinda wholesome and down-to-earth about her . . . well, except for the way she always got tongue-tied around him . . . and all the weird stuff that happened whenever she was around.

Weird stuff like—

"LOOK AT THAT!" Elizabeth Mindlessfan, Hesper's best friend since forever, cried.

Hesper turned to see a stack of sheet music on the shelf by the open window begin to blow across the room. And we're not talking a single sheet of music at a time. We're talking the entire stack—as in a foot-high pile of paper that mysteriously floated past the kids and came to a stop directly above Hesper's head.

And if that wasn't weird enough, Chad heard the New Kid whisper, "No, Herby! Herby, no!"

He watched with everybody else as the stack started to tilt.

"That's not funny!" the New Kid whispered. "Tuna, stop him!"

But whatever weird spell the New Kid was chanting made little difference. The papers slid off the stack and crashed down on top of Hesper Breakahart's head.

"Augh!" she screamed. "My expensive Beverly Hills haircut!"

Everyone in the room laughed—well, except for Hesper's wannabes, who were too busy picking up the papers and throwing them on top of their own heads, screaming, "Augh! Our expensive Beverly Hills haircuts!"

And the New Kid? She was staring off into empty space, continuing to whisper at some invisible fish

named Tuna and some imaginary friend named
Herby . . . until she caught Chad staring at her.
That's when she stopped and looked away, her
face growing even redder than before. Poor thing.
If it weren't for all that weirdness, she would be
completely sweet and normal.

* * *

Forty-five minutes later, the completely sweet and
normal TJ Finkelstein was outside, walking on the
school's track at lunchtime. She'd prefer to be inside,
eating her lunch in the lunchroom at lunchtime, but
she figured it was better to yell at her two invisible
pals from the 23rd century where no one could
overhear.

"How many times have I told you to stay at
home?" she demanded.

Herby, a tall surfer dude, floated beside her with
his legs crossed. "But if we stay at home, how can
we secretly spy on you without you knowing it?"
he asked.

TJ gave him a look. Herby's brainpower was as
bad as her singing.

"What?" he asked, flipping his bangs aside and
flexing his arm muscles. He always flipped and flexed

for TJ. (His flirting was as obvious as his lack of brain cells.)

Tuna, the smarter of the two (which is like comparing the intelligence of one tree stump to another), floated at her other side. "You must admit that Hesper Breakahart was incredibly rude to you."

"And you're going to fix that by dumping a stack of papers on her?" TJ asked.

"Actually, that was Herby's idea."

"Only because you wanted to use the Morphing Blade and turn her into an earthworm," Herby said.

TJ frowned at Tuna in disapproval. "An earthworm? Really?"

Tuna shrugged. "I was going to let her keep her pretty hair."

"Listen, guys, I really appreciate your trying to help. I can't stand Hesper any more than you. But shouldn't you be working on your time pod so you can get back to your own century? Haven't you done enough research on me for your history report?"

"We can never do enough research on the great TJ Finkelstein," Herby said, flexing his other arm.

"Remember," Tuna added, "someday you will be a great world leader."

"You keep saying that," TJ sighed. "But how can

I become a great world leader when I'm the seventh grade's worst loser?"

"Our history holographs don't lie," Tuna said. "Everything about you will be great."

"Well, except for your singing," Herby said.

TJ shook her head. "Seriously, guys, you've been here for like five months now."

Herby glanced down at his shoelace and read the time. "Actually, 105 days, 14 hours, 24 minutes, and 12 seconds."

"Right," TJ said. "But my point is—"

"Make that 105 days, 14 hours, 24 minutes, and 18 seconds." (Herby liked to be precise.)

"Thank you. What I'm trying to say is—"

"105 days, 14 hours, 24—"

Raising her voice, she repeated, "What I'm trying to say is, after all this time, shouldn't your time pod be fixed?"

"Actually," Tuna said, "that is what we have come here to discuss."

"All our repairs are done," Herby said. "Everything's de-zworked."

TJ couldn't hide her excitement. "Really?"

"Well, except for the Swiss Army knife," Herby said as he pulled it from his pocket.

"Not now," Tuna warned.

"Right." Herby opened the blade. "I'm just saying that some of the features still cause major quod-quod."

"Herby."

"Like this fingernail clipper. Instead of clipping our fingernails, it—"

"HERBY, DON'T ENGAGE THE—"

Before Tuna could finish, there was a blur of action as the Swiss Army knife leaped from Herby's hands and

BUZZ-cut . . . BUZZ-cut . . . BUZZ-cut

everything in sight. And I mean *everything*. The trees, the grass, the two 23rd-century time travelers, who were suddenly and completely

"HERBY!"

bald. And one rather unhappy seventh grader who, fearing the worst, reached up to her head and felt her brand-new do.

"GUYS!!!"

Make that her brand-new *lack of do*. That's right, TJ Finkelstein looked like a beach ball that'd just had a close shave after drinking a bottle of hair remover.

TRANSLATION: She was bald.

TJ groaned. "Terrific. Just terrific."

"Sorry." Herby shrugged.

"It will grow back," Tuna said.

"We hope," Herby added.

As they spoke, a very upset and very bald squirrel, with a very nonbushy tail, scampered over to them and chattered angrily. After giving them a piece of his mind, he turned and raced for the nearest buzz-cut tree hoping to hide among the leaves. (Good luck with that.)

TJ took a deep breath and tried her best to stay calm (a technique you learn when haunted by 23rd-century time stumblers). "You say you'll be heading home soon?"

"That is correct," Tuna said.

"Just as soon as we find fuel," Herby said while

carefully—*very* carefully—closing the blade to the knife and slipping it back into his pocket.

"And the gas station down the street won't do the trick?" TJ asked.

"Correct again," Tuna said. "As we have previously stated, we will need one plutonium power pack from a nuclear submarine, one bowl of chili from a Texas housewife . . ."

"And one flock of African ostriches to digest the chili," Herby finished.

"So how's that coming?" TJ asked.

Both boys felt a sudden need to examine the ground or the tops of their shoes or anything that didn't involve looking into her eyes.

"Guys?"

Tuna finally answered. "We have found a nuclear submarine. It's docked down at Long Beach, not too far from here."

"But . . . ?"

"It is well guarded and we can't approach it."

"But you're invisible," TJ argued. "No one can see you."

"No one but you," Herby said, flexing both arms and flipping his hair (which would have been easier if he had any hair to flip).

TJ ignored him and asked, "Okay, if you're invisible, why don't you just go to the submarine and take it?"

"You mean, 'borrow' it," Tuna corrected.

"Once we return to our century we'll send it back," Herby said.

"Okay," TJ repeated, "if you're invisible, why don't you just go in and *borrow* it?"

"Obviously," Tuna said, "because their thermal indicators will detect our radiant body signatures." (Sometimes Tuna gets a little technical.) "Which would indicate an intruder has compromised their security, thereby leading to our eventual and inevitable incarceration." (Sometimes Tuna gets *a lot* technical.)

Herby nodded. "Not only that but we'd get in trouble."

Before TJ could respond, or at least let out another groan, the ground began to

rumble . . . rumble . . . rumble . . .

under her feet.

"Do you feel that?" she asked.

"Perhaps it is a minor earthquake," Tuna said.

rumble . . . rumble . . . rumble . . .

"Or a major one," Herby said.

TJ would have agreed . . . if it weren't for the far end of the track peeling up from the ground and rising high into the air. "Uh, guys?"

His back to the track, Tuna continued, "That's another reason she should never have moved here from the Midwest."

"Yeah, dude," Herby agreed, "but what about their tornadoes?"

"You do have a point there," Tuna said.

rumble . . . rumble . . . rumble . . .

Not only was the track rising into the air, but the top of it was turning into a hideous-looking face.

"Uh, fellas?"

"If she had to move, she could have moved up north," Herby offered.

"Too much snow."

Now arms were stretching out from both sides of the rising track.

"Whoa, guys . . ."

"And the South?"

"Hurricanes."

TJ watched as legs formed, then feet, with the left one

r...i...pp......i......n.........g

away from the ground, then the right one

r...i...pp......i......n.........g

away.

So just for the record, we're talking about a piece of track, towering 30 or so feet above our heroes and wearing a rather unpleasant expression. Oh, and it talked. Let's not forget the talking.

"Hello, boys."

The voice stopped Tuna and Herby's discussion. They turned, looked up, and saw the track leering down at them. Oh, and a foot rising up to pulverize them into the ground. Let's not forget the pulverizing foot.

Tuna looked at Herby.
Herby looked at Tuna.
Then they screamed in two-part harmony:

"Bruce Bruiseabone!!"

Now, for those of you taking your first trip into
TJ's Land of Insanity, let me explain that Bruce
Bruiseabone is Tuna and Herby's archenemy. For
reasons you don't want to know (but will have
to learn in chapter two), he has come back from
the 23rd century to destroy the boys' history
report on TJ (and the boys, too, while he's at it).
And for other reasons you don't want to know,
he always shows up morphed into something big
and scary—a runaway elephant, an attacking UFO,
and this, his latest and greatest: a monster track
about to stomp them to their deaths . . . or at least
into some very bad bruises.

All of this allowed our boys to show their true
and heroic colors, which involved

"AUGH"-ing

their bald little heads off and racing away.

Needless to say (though I'm going to say it anyway), our heroes were running for their lives. But where exactly do you run from a track?

"The bleachers!" TJ shouted.

Without saying a word (unless you count hysterical yelling and screaming as words), the trio raced to the nearby bleachers and ducked underneath. Not a bad idea except wooden bleachers are no match for a 30-foot piece of track made of red crushed gravel. Red crushed gravel that

SLAM-ed

down on top of the bleachers and completely ruined them—except for the little pieces that might be useful as toothpicks. But being more in the mood for life-saving than teeth-picking, TJ looked for another escape. Spotting the school cafeteria ahead, she shouted something incredibly intelligent like

"The school cafeteria UP ahead!"

Of course Bruce was doing his own shouting. Sweet little endearments like:

"I'm going to crush you. Then I'm going to smash you. Then I'm going to eat you. . . ."

This brings up an entirely different discussion about what red-gravel tracks eat. But TJ had no time for such small talk. She thought it was a better idea to keep running as the track stomped closer and closer.

The cafeteria stood just 20 feet ahead, but the stomping grew closer.

Now the building was 10 feet away.

Red gravel began falling all around her. He was right above her head.

Finally she ducked under the cafeteria's porch roof, where she would be nice and safe.

CRASH

Okay, maybe not.

Reaching for the cafeteria door, she threw it open and stumbled inside. She turned to yank it shut but

Tuna and Herby were right behind. "Hurry up!" she yelled. "Come on!"

They finally dove through the door and TJ yanked it shut.

The good news was they were safely inside.

The bad news was the 327 students. The 327 students who stopped talking and turned to see TJ Finkelstein completely bald, yelling at two imaginary friends, and covered from head to toe with red gravel.

CHAPTER TWO

A Change of Mind(s)

TJ stood in front of her dresser mirror trying on the half-dozen hats she'd bought on the way home from school. She wasn't a big fan of hats, but she was less a fan of baldness (especially her own). In the background, Hesper Breakahart was being interviewed on the TV gossip show *Entertorment Tonight.* TJ wasn't sure why she watched it. Probably the same reason she watched scary movies and stared at car crashes along the side of the road—some things were just too horrible not to look at.

Meanwhile, the boys hovered over her desk, where Tuna was finishing up repairs on their Acme Thought Broadcaster Pen (sold at 23rd-century time-travel stores everywhere). The last couple times they'd used it had not been too successful, unless you call broadcasting your thoughts to the entire student body or thinking people into vultures and giant screaming babies successful. The point was, if the boys were serious about getting the plutonium power pack from the nuclear submarine, they'd need all their equipment to be working.

"So," TJ asked as she tossed another hat on the bed, "what exactly does this Bruce Bruiseabone have against you?"

"The dude's got a major problem with forgive-ness," Herby said.

Tuna added, "Similar in some ways to you and Hesper Breakahart."

TJ glanced at the TV, where Hesper Breakahart was rattling on about—what else?—Hesper Breakahart. TJ turned back to them and argued, "Hey, I learned my lesson. After that time on her set, I'm trying to think only good things about her."

"Really?" Tuna asked. "What good thing are you currently thinking about her?"

"Uh, um, er . . . I'm thinking it's a good thing this show is almost over."

Tuna shook his head. "Trying to think good things about someone is not the same as forgiving them."

"Why should I forgive her?" TJ said while trying on another hat. "She's made my life miserable since the first day I got here."

"'Cause if you don't, it can majorly zwork you up," Herby replied.

"Excuse me," TJ said, "am I not talking to the boy who dumped a stack of sheet music all over her head?"

"She's got a point, Herb," Tuna said.

She turned on Tuna. "Or the boy who wanted to turn her into an earthworm?"

Herby shrugged. "Sometimes we don't do what we should."

TJ arched an eyebrow. "Sometimes?"

"But *you* will," Tuna said as he returned to work on the pen. "That's what will make you the great TJ Finkelstein."

TJ shook her head. The thought of someday being

great always left her with a mixture of nervousness and excitement. Pushing up her glasses, she tried on another hat. "So tell me what happened between you and Bruce Bruiseabone."

"Well," Tuna said, "there was that incident where we accidentally blew up his locker with a neutron bomb."

Herby shrugged. "Accidents do happen."

Tuna nodded. "However, I think he resents us most for that time he was delivering a speech to the entire student body."

"What happened?" TJ asked.

Herby answered, "Well, we were always pulling pranks on each other. And the dude, he was standing onstage in front of everybody."

"And?" TJ asked.

"And for a little joke, we hit him with an Invisibility Ray."

"You made him invisible?" TJ said.

"We're not that zworked," Herby replied. "We just invisibilized his clothes."

"So he stood in front of the whole school in his underwear?" TJ asked.

"That was the idea," Tuna said. "Except Herby had some technical difficulties."

Herby shrugged. "I invisibilized *all* his clothes."

"Naked?" TJ asked in astonishment. "You made him stand in front of the whole school *naked?"*

"The whole world," Tuna corrected.

"They're still playing the video on MeTube," Herby said.

TJ stared in disbelief.

"But if he would let us explain the circumstances," Tuna said, "that things sort of got out of hand, I'm certain we could work out all of our differences."

Herby nodded. "Sometimes you gotta get inside someone's head to know what they're really thinking."

TJ chuckled. Inside Herby's head was the last place she imagined anybody would want to be . . . although there would be plenty of room to move around.

"There," Tuna said, looking up from the Thought Broadcaster Pen. "I believe it is now repaired."

"Groovy," Herby said. "Let's try it out."

Tuna lifted the pen and pointed it at Herby. He was about to fire it when he noticed TJ watching. "Actually, it is best if you look another direction," he explained.

"Why's that?" she asked.

"The beam is now configured to broadcast thoughts between two people as they look at each other."

"Oh, all right," TJ said. She turned back to the TV program.

"Hit me, bro," Herby said.

Tuna nodded and counted down. "Three . . . two . . . one . . ."

TJ heard the usual

zibwaaa . . . zibwaaa . . . zibwaaa

of the beam being fired. Followed by the not-so-usual

TINKA . . .

DOINK-DOINK-DOINK

"Uh-oh," Herby said.

"That can't be good," Tuna agreed.

And with every

TINKA . . .

the

DOINK-DOINK-DOINK

grew louder.

"What's going on?" Herby shouted over the noise.

Tuna answered, "The electrical signal from the television broadcast is drawing the beam to the TV set!"

"And that's what's wrong?" Herby asked.

TINKA . . .

"No. That's what's—"

DOINK-DOINK-DOINK

TERRIBLE!"

Before TJ could turn from the TV to see the problem, the beam struck the screen where Hesper was talking and bounced directly into TJ's eyes.

The good news was the stupid sound effects finally disappeared.

The bad news was . . . so did TJ.

Well, she didn't disappear, not really. I mean, TJ was still there. Only now she was looking around the room, more than a little surprised.

"What's going on?" she demanded. "Where's my camera?"

"Uh-oh," Herby repeated.

She turned toward Herby's voice. "Who's there? Where are you?"

"Can't you see us?" Herby asked.

The girl stiffened, obviously frightened, as she searched in vain for them. "Where are you? Who are you?"

The boys glanced nervously at each other. Finally Tuna cleared his throat. "Actually, the question is, who are you?"

Her eyes continued darting around the room. "How did I get in this awful dressing room?" It was about this time she spotted the dresser mirror. And it was about this time she let out the world's third-loudest

"AUUUUUUUUUUUGH!!"

scream.

The runner-up and the world's loudest scream would come a moment later, but right now she had to get through the yelling part: "What have you done to my hair? And my body?" Turning to look at herself in profile, she shouted, "My trainer is going to hear about this!"

Tuna tried to interrupt, but she was too busy having a panic attack to pay attention.

"And my face!" She reached up and touched her cheeks. "What have you done to my delicate bone structure, my beautiful skin?" Then she saw her hands.

"AuuuUUUuuuugh!!!"

(Hang on; it will get louder.)

"My beautiful, manicured fingers? And—"

"AuuuUUUuuuugh!!!!"

(There we go.)

"A BROKEN NAIL. I'VE GOT A BROKEN NAIL!"

Filled with rage, she spun back toward the voices and shouted, "I WANT TO SEE MY AGENT, AND I WANT TO SEE HIM NOW!"

Then, spotting the TV, she gasped. Tuna and

Herby watched as she stepped closer to the screen.
Hesper Breakahart was still giving her interview. But
instead of answering questions with her usual snooty
attitude, she wasn't answering them with anything.
Including her voice. The TV star was so terrified she
could no longer speak.

"WHAT'S GOING ON?!" the girl in TJ's room
shouted at the TV set. "WHAT AM I DOING HERE,
WHEN I'M REALLY THERE?"

The boys exchanged glances.

Tuna cleared his throat and asked the obvious
question. "And who exactly are you?"

"Don't be ridiculous. Everybody knows who
I am!"

"Right, but just for fun, if someone were to ask,
what would you tell them?"

She pointed at the TV screen. "I'd tell them
I'm her!"

"Who?"

"I'M HESPER BREAKAHART!"

* * *

Meanwhile, TJ—the real TJ—was enjoying her own
set of migraine makers. Because no matter how
much you've been shocked by goofy time travelers

from the 23rd century, there's still something a little surprising about finding yourself transported into someone else's body.

TRANSPORTED INTO SOMEONE ELSE'S BODY?!

I'm yelling again; sorry. But TJ would have yelled too, if she could have found her voice. Like I said, things were a little surprising—though it was nice having hair again, even if it was the wrong color and belonged to somebody else.

And what was with the tightness she felt around her waist? As discreetly as possible, TJ slipped her hands down to her tummy and felt . . . Was it possible? Was the perfect Hesper Breakahart wearing a girdle?! No wonder she always had such a flat stomach—it was held in by a giant elastic bandage! Wait until she told the kids back at—

Wait a minute—there were no kids she could tell back at school. There were no kids she could tell anywhere. No one would believe her. To be honest, *she* wasn't sure she believed her.

"So tell us, Hesper—" the smiley-faced TV reporter clapped her hands eagerly—"after your wonderful outreach to the homeless last Christmas, what are your plans now?"

TJ blinked at the bright lights as she glanced around the TV studio.

The reporter waited.

TJ blinked some more.

The reporter waited some more.

Off to the left TJ spotted Hesper's manager, Bernie Makeabuck. He was on his cell phone, wheeling and dealing like always.

To her right she saw Hesper's hairstylist, armed with two curling irons, three hairbrushes, and a year's supply of hair spray . . . in each hand. Beside her stood the makeup lady holding a dozen tubes of concealer, three powder puffs, and more lipsticks than a Bags Fifth Avenue cosmetics counter. Behind them stood Elizabeth Mindlessfan along with all of Hesper's other wannabes, hanging on every word TJ was too stunned to speak.

All right, enough was enough. Whatever the boys had done, it was time to stop this nightmare and get back home. So as softly as possible, she whispered, "Tuna? Herby? Get me out of here."

"I'm sorry," the smiley-faced reporter said. "What was that?"

TJ tried to smile back but her smiler was as

stunned as her talker. Then, just when things couldn't get any worse, she heard the ever-dreaded

chugga-chugga-chugga

BLING!

which is the sound all 23rd-century Transporter Blades make when transporting 23rd-century time travelers.

Suddenly there were Herby and Tuna, floating at her side—invisible to everyone but TJ.

"Hey there, Your Dude-ness," Herby whispered.

She whispered back, "Nice of you to drop by."

"I'm sorry?" the reporter said.

Tuna whispered into TJ's other ear, "Apparently we had a little glitch with the Thought Broadcaster Pen."

TJ threw him a look. "You think?"

Herby whispered, "I bet you'd like to get back into your own body, huh?"

"Yeah, being in my own body would be very nice," TJ said.

The smiley-faced reporter glanced about and fidgeted nervously.

"We've just got one minor problem," Herby whispered.

"Which is?"

"Hesper Breakahart's in it."

"WHAT?" TJ shouted.

The smiley-faced reporter's smile began to twitch. "I'm sorry, Hesper. Is there a problem?"

TJ shouted at Tuna, "HESPER BREAKAHART'S IN MY BODY?"

"Well, yes," the reporter stammered. "Where else would you be?"

"AND WHERE IS MY BODY?" TJ demanded.

"I'm sorry?" The reporter looked more confused than ever.

"Not to worry, Your Dude-ness," Herby whispered. "It's all tied up nice and neatly in the bathroom."

"MY BODY'S TIED UP IN MY BATHROOM?!"

"I beg your pardon?" The smiley-faced reporter was no longer smiling.

"Uh, not *your* bathroom," Tuna whispered. "That would be too easy to find."

"It's in a bathroom on the International Space Station," Herby explained.

"MY BODY'S TIED UP IN A BATHROOM ON THE INTERNATIONAL SPACE STATION?!"

The reporter looked around, frightened.

"This is a joke, right?" TJ asked.

Relief washed over the reporter's face as she tried to giggle. "Oh, so you're making a joke."

"I wish it was," Tuna sighed.

"It's no joke?" TJ asked.

"It's no joke?" the reporter asked.

TJ turned to the reporter, not understanding what the woman was talking about.

"Your body being tied up in the International Space Station's bathroom?" the reporter said. "You're not making a joke?"

TJ slowly, sadly, shook her head.

"I see." The reporter hesitated, then leaned forward and softly asked, "So tell us, Ms. Breakahart . . . how long have you been battling this secret mental condition?"

CHAPTER THREE

Superstar Grande, Nonfat, Heavy on the Ice

TIME TRAVEL LOG:

Malibu, California, January 23—supplemental

Begin Transmission:

Tuna had a brainstorm. (In his case more like a brain squall.) In any case, the dude thought a cool thought, which was better than thinking no thought. At least that's what we thought.

End Transmission

TJ had barely finished the interview before Bernie, Hesper's manager, began dragging her toward the stage door. "Don't worry, babe," he said. "We all say stupid things."

Before TJ could explain she wasn't actually the babe he thought she was (and that saying stupid things was her specialty), he continued, "The point is we can play this up big, *big, big!* I can see the headline now: 'TV Star Has Mental Meltdown.' Fantastic, babe, absolutely brilliant!"

As he spoke, TJ was looking over her shoulder, trying to find the boys. "Tuna? Herby?"

"Oh, that's great. You're magic, babe. You'll make the gossip shows for weeks. Big, *big, big!*" One of his three cell phones rang and he answered it. "Talk to me!" As he spoke, he snapped his fingers for a stagehand to open the back door for them (since he was obviously too important to do it himself).

The door opened and TJ stepped into a crowd of screaming fans.

"OH, HESPER, WE LOVE YOU!"
"OH, HESPER, WILL YOU SIGN MY AUTOGRAPH BOOK?"
"OH, HESPER, WILL YOU SIGN MY FACE?"

TJ wanted to be nice, so even though it was kinda, sorta, in a waya forgery, she reached for a pen and started signing Hesper's name. The crowd pressed in closer.

"OH, HESPER, WE LOVE YOU!"
"OH, HESPER, CAN I TOUCH YOUR SHIRT?"
"OH, HESPER, CAN I HAVE THIS

ripPPPPP . . .

PIECE OF YOUR SHIRT?"

"Hey!" TJ cried.

"OH, HESPER, WE LOVE YOU!"
"OH, HESPER, CAN I HAVE THIS

ripPPPPP . . .

PIECE OF YOUR HAIR?"

"Ow!"

But no one cared how TJ felt. They were too busy loving her . . . until Bernie grabbed her arm and yanked her into the limousine. But not before she lost a couple more pieces of

ripPPPPP . . .

"BRRR . . ."

clothing and several more handfuls of

riPPPPPP ...

"YEOW!"

hair.

Once they were inside, he slammed the limo door and they sped off. Not, of course, without running over a few of her

"OH, HESPER, WE LOVE—"

adoring fans'

crunch, crunch, crunch

"AUGH! AUGH! AUGH!"

tootsies.

TJ was hoping to finally catch her breath. And she could have, if it weren't for the 6,000-year-old secretary with bleached blonde hair, 7 shades of eye shadow, and 4½ pounds of mascara who started giving her instructions:

"We've got plenty more appointments tonight, so listen up."

TJ glanced at her watch. "But it's 9:15."

"Exactly—we're already behind schedule."

Another woman, who had more muscles than Coach Steroidson (and could have used some of the secretary's makeup), sat across from TJ and ordered, "Getz down on zee floor."

"I'm sorry, what?"

"For your zit-upz," she said. "You haf not done your 2,500 zit-upz for zee day. Getz down und getz ztarted!"

TJ threw a look to Bernie, who was still on his phones.

"Getz down! Getz down!"

Reluctantly, TJ lowered herself to the floor.

"Und up."

TJ hesitated.

"Up." The woman motioned for her to sit up. "Up, up!"

TJ sat up.

"Und down."

She lay back down.

"Und up. Fazter."

TJ sat up more quickly.

"Und down. Fazter. Fazter!"

As TJ continued her sit-ups, the secretary began reading the schedule. "We have a photo op with Brad Spit in just twenty minutes. Do try not to drool this time."

"Und up, und down. Fazter, fatty. Fazter!"

TJ sat up faster.

"And the crew's all set to start filming your Choka-Cola ad in the ocean at one o'clock."

"In the ocean?" TJ asked, trying to catch her breath. "At one in the morning? It'll be freezing."

"Fazter, tubby tummy!"

Bernie glanced up from his phone. "Don't worry, babe. We'll airbrush out all your goose bumps."

The secretary nodded. "And Photoshop will fix that awful blue color you turn whenever you get frostbite."

"Und up! Und down!"

"When do I sleep?" TJ asked, gasping for air.

"Sleep?" The secretary laughed. "You're a star. You don't have time to sleep."

"Not to worry, babe," Bernie said. "We have plenty of coffee to keep you awake. And so it doesn't stain those expensive teeth of yours . . ." He snapped his fingers at the secretary and she produced an IV drip bag like they use in hospitals. But instead of medicine it was full of coffee.

Before TJ could protest, the woman shoved the needle into her arm.

"Ow!"

"You're zlowing down, chunky chick," the trainer barked. "Und up, und down, und up . . ."

TJ couldn't believe what was happening. She had no idea Hesper lived this kind of life (or lack of one). "Can we stop by a McDonald's?" she asked between breaths. "I'm starving."

All three adults broke out laughing.

"What's so funny?"

"You haf already had your carrot ztick for zee day."

"I'm afraid she's right," the secretary said. "And with that bikini you'll be wearing tonight, every ounce counts."

"Fazter, jelly belly," the trainer yelled. "Fazter, fazter!"

"Perfect!" Bernie said, snapping his phone shut with a flair. "We have you all set to go in for a mental evaluation."

"Mental evaluation?" TJ asked.

"Yeah, isn't that great?"

"But I'm okay!" TJ protested.

"We know that and you know that." Bernie broke into a grin. "We just have to make sure the press doesn't."

"You *want* them to think I'm crazy?"

"Just until the world thinks you are." His grin widened. Another one of his phones rang and he answered. "Talk to me."

Amazing. So this was what went on behind the scenes in Hesper Breakahart's life. No wonder she was so mean and cranky.

"No, you can't speak to her!" Bernie shouted into the phone. "You spoke to her just last week! And if you try to contact her again, I'll have you arrested for stalking, do you understand? Good-bye!"

"Another fan?" the secretary asked.

"I wish it was that simple," Bernie grumbled. Looking at TJ, he said, "It's your mother again."

For a moment, TJ's heart leaped. But of course, it wasn't *her* mother. Her mother was dead, taken from them by cancer a year ago. Not a day went by that she didn't miss her. But Hesper's mother was alive. Alive and trying to talk with her daughter. And they wouldn't let her? What type of people were these?

"You're stopping Hesper's mom from talking to her?" TJ asked.

Bernie didn't bother answering.

TJ tried again. "Would you really put her in jail?"

"And throw away the key," Bernie said as he

dialed another number. "You're far too busy to be bothered by somebody like that."

Once again TJ's heart went out to Hesper. Was this really what her life was like?

All this as the trainer barked, "Fazter, fatzo! Und up, und down. Fazter! Fazter!"

*　*　*

TJ was colder than an ice cube in a freezer in Antarctica . . . on a cloudy day. Although she was used to extreme temperatures (hey, she's from the Midwest), there's something about standing . . .

　　—in the middle of the Pacific Ocean
　　—in the middle of the night
　　—in the middle of winter

that can make a person a little chilly . . . especially if she's forced to wear a dental-floss bikini.

TJ knew Hesper would throw a fit, so she tried her best to throw one herself. Unfortunately, the best she had was a polite

　　"Uh, excuse me, if it's not too much bother, will we be done anytime soon?"

　　(Like I said, she's from the Midwest.)

And no matter how she complained (or didn't), Hesper's manager always had the same answers:

"Trust me—this is important, babe."
"Trust me—there's money here, babe."
"Trust me—I'm making you a superstar, babe."

Then of course there were the 73 reporters standing on the beach waiting to interview the "TV STAR GONE CRAZY."

Oh, and let's not forget the director, who was on the nice, dry beach, bundled in nice, warm blankets.

"Perfect," he shouted after take 150. (Which was the same thing he shouted after the other 149 takes.) "You're beautiful. You're gorgeous. The camera loves you. Let's try one more, this time without all that teeth-chattering." (He'd said that for the past 149 takes too.)

To be honest, TJ didn't have to do much acting. All she had to do was take a sip from the Choka-Cola can, smile at the camera, and say one word: "Yum!"

Unfortunately, when she took a sip from the can and smiled at the camera, all she could say was, "Y-y-y-y-yum."

But this time it would be different. Take 151 would be the winner.

And it might have been if TJ hadn't heard the all-too-familiar

Chugga-chugga-chugga

which, of course, is the sound all 23rd-century Transporter Blades make when transporting 23rd-century time travelers

BLING!

directly beside you.

"What's happenin', Your Dude-ness?"

She turned to see Herby floating above the water . . . though he looked more like a polar bear with all the fur coats he was wearing.

"Wh-wh-where have you b-b-b-been?" she shivered.

"Down at the local Dairy Queen," he answered. Only then did she notice the ice cream cone he was eating—chocolate, triple dip.

"An extremely tasty place," Tuna said, floating at her other side. He gave a loud

sluuuuuuuurp

of the giant slush he was drinking—cherry flavored,
light on the ice.

"W-w-wonderful," TJ muttered.

"Hey, we didn't forget you," Herby said as he
produced a caramel and fudge sundae for her.

"N-n-no th-th-thank you."

"Allergic to dairy products?" Tuna asked.

"N-n-no." She shook her head. "J-j-just stupidity."

The boys gave each other a look, shrugged, then
resumed eating.

After a few slurps, Tuna spoke up. "Herby and
I believe we have discovered a solution to our
problem."

"Your p-p-problem? What about m-m-mine?"

"You mean that stutter?" Herby asked.

"They have doctors who can help with that,"
Tuna said.

TJ wanted to roll her eyes, but she was afraid
they'd freeze up in her head. Instead she said,
"Y-y-you have a s-s-s-solution?"

"Oh, right—" Herby nodded—"a solution." He
hesitated, scowled, and turned to Tuna. "What was
it again?"

Tuna gave a sigh, took another

siuuuuuuuurp

then patiently explained, "Hesper Breakahart is a big-time star, right?"

"Right," Herby answered.

"And big-time stars always do benefits for the troops, right?"

"Right."

"So there you have it."

Herby grinned and turned to TJ. "So there we have it."

"Have wh-wh-what?" TJ asked.

Herby turned to Tuna. "Have what?"

Tuna gave another sigh, took another

siuuuuuuuurp

and explained, "As Hesper Breakahart, all you have to do is offer to put on a benefit concert for the sailors on the pier by the nuclear submarine. As you're performing, we'll sneak into the sub, steal the plutonium power pack, and there we go."

Herby grinned and nodded to TJ. "And there we go."

Naturally, TJ wanted to ask a question or two. Nothing complicated, just something simple like

"HAVE YOU TWO LOST YOUR MINDS?!"

But Tuna kept on talking. "Of course, we'll need the help of a couple of your friends."

"Of course." Herby nodded, then stopped. "She has friends?"

Before TJ could point out that she might have more if it weren't for their constant "help," the commercial director shouted from the shore, "Quiet on the set, please!"

Tuna leaned into TJ's ear and whispered, "As soon as you're done fooling around here, we'll meet up and work out a plan." He nodded to Herby, who pulled out the Transporter Blade from his Swiss Army knife.

"Wh-wh-where are you going?" TJ whispered.

Tuna gave one last

sluuuuuuuurp

and answered, "Back to the Dairy Queen."

"You sure you don't want anything?" Herby asked.

The very thought made TJ shiver harder as Herby pressed the blade

Chugga-chugga-chugga

and the director shouted

BLING!

"Action!"

CHAPTER FOUR

Want to Know a Secret?

Too bad; I'll tell it anyway

TIME TRAVEL LOG:

Malibu, California, January 24

Begin Transmission:

Tuna and I made new friends. Of course, it
would be more fun if they didn't always scream,
run away, or pass out. Not entirely sure of the
reason. Perhaps I'll start bathing . . . maybe use
deodorant.

End Transmission

The Choka-Cola commercial ended just in time for
TJ to start school. She had barely dragged herself into
the hallway before she was surrounded by the usual

Hesper wannabes with their usual Hesper-wannabe concerns:

"Oh, Hesper, are you all right?"

"Oh, Hesper, we were so worried."

Then there was the queen mother of all wannabes, Elizabeth Mindlessfan, Hesper's best friend since forever (at least according to Elizabeth). Not only did she dress and fix her hair like Hesper, but this morning she kept looking over her shoulder and whispering to her imaginary friends . . . just like Hesper.

"Leave me alone, Salmon," she hissed. (At least she got the fish part right—sorta.)

"What are you doing?" TJ asked her.

"No, I'm not going back to the space station," Elizabeth shouted over her other shoulder.

Herby, who was floating beside TJ, whispered, "What's with her?"

"She's talking to us," Tuna answered from TJ's other side.

"But we're over here." Herby glanced around in confusion. "Aren't we?"

"Hey, Hesper," a voice called. "Hesper!"

At first TJ didn't realize it was calling to her.

Finally she turned to see Chad Steel approaching. Not only was he approaching but he was speaking . . . to her. (Insert gulp here.) But who knows, now that she was in Hesper's body, maybe she could actually talk to him without getting tongue-tied.

"H . . . h . . . hi," she answered. (Maybe not.)

Chad tilted his head and looked at her with those incredible blue eyes. But before she could pass out—or at least run to the bathroom and throw up—she heard another familiar voice.

"I know this is some stupid dream, but I want to wake up and I want to wake up now!"

TJ turned to see . . . well, to see herself storming down the hallway. I mean, it was the same bean-pole body, the same glasses, and let's not forget the latest in shaved heads, courtesy of Herby's fingernail clipper. It was definitely TJ's body but definitely *not* her voice . . . or her personality. Truth is, there's only person on earth who could have such a cranky personality. And yet, after all TJ had been through in the past 12 hours, she was actually starting to understand why Hesper was so hard to get along with.

"Just look at my skin!" Hesper shouted. "And these nails! And these clothes! Everything's so . . . so . . . ordinary! This isn't a dream; it's a nightmare!"

The good news was the boys had obviously

transported her back from the International Space Station. The bad news was, well, the boys had obviously transported her back from the International Space Station.

"She thinks she's dreaming?" TJ whispered.

"Wouldn't you?" Tuna said.

TJ sighed. "I wish."

At last, Hesper spotted TJ and screamed, "MY HAIR! LOOK AT MY HAIR!"

TJ ran a self-conscious hand through her hair. Thanks to the on-call hairstylist, it was nearly perfect. But as we all know by now, when it comes to Hesper's looks, *nearly* is never perfect enough.

"THERE'S A STRAND OUT OF PLACE!" she screamed.

Of course, all of Hesper's wannabes pulled out strands from their own hair. "Oh no, our hair!" they shouted. "It's out of place! It's out of place!"

If that's not confusing enough (and believe me, we've just started), TJ's friends, Doug Claudlooper (aka the allergy king) and Naomi Simpletwirp (the gold medalist in breath-mint chewing), appeared in the hallway and approached Hesper (who they thought was TJ).

"Hey, TJ," Naomi called out to her, "you okay?"

Hesper paid no attention. All she could do was keep screaming, "MY HAIR! LOOK AT MY HAIR!"

"Yeah, I *(sniff-sniff)* know," Doug said. "I don't think bald is really your look."

"NOT *MY* HAIR, YOU LOSER!" Hesper shouted. She pointed at TJ. "*MY* HAIR!"

Chad leaned toward TJ and asked, "What's with the New Kid?"

Before TJ found her voice (and with Chad that could take a century or two), Elizabeth answered, "She's just jealous." Then she turned sweetly to TJ. "Everyone loves your hair, Hesper."

"Oh yes," the wannabes chimed in. "We love your hair—love, love, love."

"Uh, Tuna?" TJ whispered. "Herby?"

"'Sup, Your Dude-ness?"

"Is it just me, or is this getting way too weird?"

"I WANT THIS NIGHTMARE TO STOP!" Hesper screamed as she stomped her dainty little foot (which in reality was TJ's big, clumsy one).

"No," Herby agreed. "On the Weirdness Scale of 1 to 10, this is definitely an 11½." (Herby's never been real good with numbers.)

"Relax, TJ," Naomi said to Hesper as she took her hand. "I don't know what your problem is, but—"

"DON'T TOUCH ME!" Hesper screamed. "WHO GAVE YOU PERMISSION TO TOUCH ME?"

Yes, sir, most definitely an 11½.

Turning back to the boys, TJ whispered, "So do you guys have a plan for fixing this mess?"

"Absolutely," Tuna said.

"Absolutely," Herby agreed.

TJ waited, but no one spoke.

Finally she said, "And if I were to ask you, would you know what that plan is?"

"Absolutely," Tuna said.

"Absolutely," Herby agreed.

More waiting.

"Tuna?" TJ asked.

"Yes?"

"The plan?"

"Right, the plan." Clearing his throat, and always happy to be in charge, Tuna began. "First, my assistant, Herby here, will produce the Thought Broadcaster Pen."

Herby fumbled in his pocket until he pulled out the pen.

"Is it fixed?" TJ asked.

"Temporarily," Tuna said.

"As long as we treat it delicately," Herby added.

Tuna continued, "Next, Herby will point the pen at—"

But that was as far as the plan went. Because there's something about a floating pen suddenly appearing before a dozen students in a hallway that causes the eyes of those students to widen, their mouths to open, and their voices to

"LOOK AT THAT!"
"WHAT IS IT?"
(Great, just what we need—more screaming.)

Of course, helpful Herby was happy to explain. "It's a 23rd-century Acme Thought Broadcaster Pen."

Unfortunately, helpful Herby forgot he was invisible, which led to even more

"WHO SAID THAT?"

screaming and more helpful answers from Herby: "Me."

The mysterious floating pen and an invisible (though very helpful) Herby brought the crowd to the only logical conclusion:

"IT'S A GHOST!"

"Where?!" Tuna shouted.

"TWO GHOSTS!!"

Everyone ran for their lives, which involved more hysterical screaming as well as lots of slamming and bumping into one another . . . including slamming and bumping into Herby . . . which caused him to drop the pen.

No problem, except for the part where Chad bent down, picked up the pen, and looked at it. Even that wouldn't be a problem if he hadn't pressed the clicker, causing the dreaded blue beam to

zibwaaa . . . zibWaaa . . . zibwaaa

shoot out and strike him in the face.

And even *that* wouldn't be a problem if Doug hadn't shouted, "What is it?" causing Chad to glance up and look directly into Doug's eyes.

TINKA . . .

DOINK-DOINK-DOINK

Okay, now we've got a problem.

* * *

Ten minutes later Chad Steel was sniffing and sneezing just like Doug Claudlooper. The reason was obvious . . .

(I will not shout, I will not shout, I will not shout . . .)
He WAS Doug Claudlooper! (My bad.)

And yes, Doug Claudlooper was now the awesome, every-girl's-dreamboat Chad Steel.

The good news was the two boys took the news a lot better than Hesper. The bad news was "a lot better than Hesper" isn't exactly the same as "well."

After everyone had scattered from the ghosts and the floating pen, TJ motioned the two guys into an empty classroom to explain. And as you might expect, they answered with a cool and calm—

"WHAT?!" Doug shouted.

"A Thought Broadcaster Pen," TJ answered.

"FROM WHERE?!" Chad demanded.

(May I point out that they're doing the shouting, not me?)

"From the, uh . . ." TJ cleared her throat. "The 23rd century."

The boys stared at her like she'd lost her mind.

She smiled back at them like she had.

Suddenly Doug spotted the reflection of his new face and new body in the window. Other than being about six inches taller and a hundred times more handsome, there wasn't much difference. "And you're absolutely certain this isn't a dream?" he asked.

"I wish it was," TJ sighed.

"I don't know," he said, running his hands through his thick, dark hair. "If I had to, I suppose I could get used to this."

Chad's reaction was slightly different. "I can't believe this is *(sniff-sniff)* happening," he said as he slumped against the door. (You'd slump too, if you were stuck in Doug's body.) "It's just too crazy."

"Welcome to my world," TJ mumbled.

Chad fought back another sneeze and sniffed a louder *SNIFF*. "You guys got a tissue or something? My nose is running like a faucet."

"Use the back of my hand," Doug answered. "I always do."

Chad glanced at his new hand and noticed its back was covered in a slippery glaze. He lowered it, making a mental note never to let it get near the rest of his body.

"So—" Doug turned from his reflection in the window to face TJ—"you're actually TJ Finkelstein, but you're living inside Hesper Breakahart's body."

"I'm afraid so," TJ said.

As Doug stared at her, he got a funny twinkle in his eyes. Then he started to smile.

"What?" she asked.

Slowly and ever so suavely Doug approached her. "So in a way, you and me . . . we're like boyfriend and girlfriend now, aren't we?" He reached toward her hand.

"Not a chance, Doug."

He frowned.

"You're dating Naomi, remember?"

"Right, sorry," he said. "Don't know what I was thinking."

Meanwhile, Chad was still slumping against the door trying to think things through. "And who exactly was it that gave you this pen?" he asked.

TJ swallowed and answered, "I'm afraid that's the part you won't believe."

"Actually," Chad said, pushing up his newly acquired glasses, complete with masking tape to hold them together, "I'm (sniff-sniff) having a hard time believing any of this." He felt another sneeze coming and tried to hold it back, but with no

"AH-CHOO!"

success.

"God bless you, dude," a voice said from beside him.

"What?" Chad spun around. "Who said that?!"

TJ dropped her head into her hands and mumbled, "That's the part you won't believe."

The two guys watched in amazement as a tissue materialized before their eyes and floated across the room toward Chad.

"Herby," a second voice whispered. "What are you doing?"

"The dude needs to blow his nose," the first voice answered.

The tissue hovered in front of Chad until, ever so cautiously, he reached out and took it. And always polite, he said, "Uh . . . thank you."

"You're welcome," the voice answered.

"Herby!"

TJ shook her head in disbelief, then raised it and called out to the voices, "Boys?"

"Who's she talking to?" the first voice whispered.

"Who do you think?" the second voice whispered back.

"Not us."

"And why not?"

"Because we're supposed to be a secret."

"You might have considered that before you performed your floating-tissue routine."

"I was just being helpful."

Chad and Doug traded looks of alarm.

"Oh, boys," TJ repeated. "Don't look now, but I think your little secret's out."

"Uh-oh," the first voice whispered, "we're in deep quod-quod now."

"See what you did," the second voice answered.

"What I did? Dude, you did it."

"I most certainly did not."

"Boys . . . ," TJ called.

"Did too."

"Did not."

"Too."

"I know you are but what am I."

"That makes no sense."

"You make no sense."

"BOYS!"

Suddenly the room grew very quiet. Not a sound could be heard . . . well, except for Chad's continual

sniff-sniff-sniff-ing

and another

"AH-CHOO!"

"He should really take something for that," the first voice said.

"Come out, come out, wherever you are," TJ called.

Chad spotted a Swiss Army knife as it appeared in the air . . . with more blades than he had ever seen. Strange blades, like the one opening in front of him now. The one making the very strange

bim-bo-bo-bo-bo-bo

sound, along with a rather bright and annoying

FLASH

of light.

The next thing Chad knew, there were two teenage boys from the 23rd century before him.

They had decloaked themselves and were casually floating in the middle of the room.

Chad slumped back against the door and gave a sad, mournful *SNIFF.* Usually he was an upbeat guy, but for some reason he was not fond of losing both his body and his mind on the same day.

Little did he know the fun and games had barely begun.

CHAPTER FIVE

Seafood Sees Food

TIME TRAVEL LOG:

Malibu, California, January 24–supplemental

Begin Transmission:

Tuna thought out his new and improved plan to get us home. It's majorly gonzo except for the usual problems: it's Tuna's plan, and it involves Tuna's thinking.

End Transmission

It took the entire first period of school to explain to Chad and Doug all of TJ's wonderful headaches. (Which is pretty good, considering it's taken us four books.)

And why did they explain all these wonderful headaches, you ask?

(You are asking, right?)

"Because," Tuna said, "I have devised a plan that will call for assistance from both of you."

"Oh, really?" Chad sniffed.

"Oh, cool," Doug exclaimed.

"Oh no," TJ moaned.

Tuna continued, "In order to secure that plutonium fuel pack from the nuclear submarine, we'll need all the help we can get."

"I think this might get interesting," Chad sniffed.

"I think it'll be exciting," Doug agreed.

"I think I'm going to get sick," TJ groaned.

Then, ever so carefully, Tuna laid out his new and improved plan (as opposed to his old and failed ones). And even though TJ vividly recalled all his past mistakes, she made an even bigger one by saying, "Sure, what have we got to lose?"

(The biggest mistake was not waiting for an answer.)

In any case, here was the plan:

STEP ONE

TJ was to set up a news conference right after school.

"How do I do that?" she asked.

"Everyone thinks you're Hesper Breakahart, right?"

"Right."

"So call your agent and demand one," Tuna said.

"What if he says no?"

"Then you throw a fit."

"I'm really not so good at that."

"Listen," Chad said, "if you're going to live inside Hesper's body, you've got to act like Hesper."

"But she's had 13 years of practice."

"But I know just how she does it." Chad grinned and TJ felt her insides get all fluttery (though, technically, they were not her insides and, technically, it was not Chad's grin). "Meet me in the choir room at lunchtime," he said. "I'll give you some quick lessons."

And three hours later, that's exactly what happened.

TJ couldn't believe it. She was alone with Chad Steel. Granted, it would have been better if he looked like Chad Steel, but some of Chad was better than none of Chad. Besides, if he was in Doug's body, maybe she could make believe it was Doug and say something semi-intelligent. (Hey, it doesn't hurt to dream.)

"Okay, try this," Chad said. He scrunched up his

face, stomped his foot, and shouted, **"ME! IT'S ALL ABOUT ME!"**

TJ nodded, tapped her foot, and squeaked, "Me. It's all about me . . . if that's okay with you."

Chad chuckled. "No, try it again." He stomped his foot and shouted, **"ME!"**

TJ tapped her foot and whispered, "Me."

He shook his head. **"ME!"**

"Me."

Chad laughed. "Well, that's a little better. This is going to take some practice. You're just too nice to be Hesper."

TJ felt her face growing hot. "Sorry."

"Sorry? No, that's a compliment. There's a lot she could learn from you."

TJ's heart skipped a beat (actually it skipped more beats than she could count). But instead of melting into a little puddle of girl goo, she felt this strange need to defend Hesper.

"She's really not so bad," she said, "considering all the pressure she's under." TJ was shocked. Not only had she spoken an entire sentence in front of Chad Steel, but she actually felt good defending Hesper. Of course she would have felt better if Chad hadn't been so quick to agree.

"Exactly," he said. "That's what I keep trying to tell people."

They continued practicing through the entire lunch period until TJ was good enough (or bad enough) to call up Hesper's manager and demand a press conference that afternoon in front of the school.

Bernie Makeabuck agreed. He didn't know what she was going to say, but it didn't matter. Crazy or not, he didn't care. Because as all great managers know . . . the only bad press coverage is no press coverage.

So far, so good. Now on to . . .

STEP TWO
After your manager arranges a news conference, there's only one problem.
You have to hold it.

No problem if you're a megastar used to being in front of the cameras every day. Big problem if you're a shy girl from Missouri who can barely stand having your school photo taken (especially when it's always your worst hair day and your parents insist on choosing the one with the goofiest smile. Oh, and let's not forget the ginormous zit that always shows up somewhere on your face that very morning.)

As soon as the last bell rang, TJ stood on the school's front lawn in front of 127 reporters, holding a speech Tuna had written. She planned to deliver it just as soon as she finished answering such sensitive and thoughtful questions as

"Ms. Breakahart, what does crazy feel like?"
"Ms. Breakahart, have you started drooling yet?"
"Ms. Breakahart, in the event of your death, will your loved ones be provided for?"

The last question stopped everyone cold, until they realized a life insurance salesman had slipped into the crowd and was trying to sell her a policy.

Once they grabbed him and threw him off the lawn into the busy

HONK . . . HONK

SQUEAL . . . SQUEAL

street (let's hope *he's* got life insurance), TJ began reading Tuna's speech.

For you guy-type readers, I'll spare you all the sappy romance parts . . . like how TJ was so shy that she sputtered and stuttered until she looked into Chad's dreamy eyes and somehow found the courage to continue. Instead, I'll just cut to the part where TJ said:

". . . and to show my appreciation to the armed forces, I will perform a free benefit concert for all the sailors at the Long Beach pier."

Oh, and I'll also spare you the part where Bernie screamed, "Free? Did she say free? I CAN'T BELIEVE SHE SAID FREE!"

But I won't spare the part where a giant crab (if you call 15 feet tall *giant*) with sunglasses scurried up the beach to the school. And how, when spotting the crowd on the front lawn, it

scurry, scurry, scurry-ed

directly at them.

Nor will I spare you how those sensitive, thoughtful reporters trampled over each other, screaming sensitive, thoughtful things like:

"GET OUT OF MY WAY!"
"WE'RE ALL GOING TO DIE!"

"WHERE'S THAT LIFE INSURANCE SALESMAN?!"

Then there was Tuna's and Herby's comment. Very simple and to the point:

"BRUCE BRUISEABONE!!!"

The good news was that Herby, one of the heroes of our story (yeah, I know, that's stretching the term *hero* a bit), immediately did what all 23rd-century heroes did . . . he reopened his Transporter Blade

chugga-chugga-chugga

and

BLING!

disappeared, along with Tuna, as fast as their cowardly little hearts could disappear.

The bad news was the 15-foot crab didn't disappear.

The badder news was (I know that's not a real word, but since when are 15-foot crabs real? Unless, of course, you're watching one of those old, black-and-white sci-fi movies.) Anyway, the badder news was TJ didn't disappear.

Come to think of it, neither did Chad or Doug. And being new to the everyday weirdness of TJ Finkelstein, they just sort of stood around screaming, "WHAT DO WE DO? WHAT DO WE DO?"

But being an old pro at this sort of stuff, TJ took a moment to think over the situation. And after carefully considering the possibilities, she calmly pointed out the only solution she could think of:

"RUN!"

And run they did—down the sidewalk toward the school.

Unfortunately, so did the 15-foot crab. Well, not run, really. With all those claws and spiny little feet on the concrete, it was more like it

click, click, CLICK, click-ed

The kids arrived at the front of the school, threw open the glass doors, and raced inside.

The crab arrived at the front of the school and

CRASH!-ed

through the glass doors. (Though he still had to suck in his little crab tummy to make it through. Obviously it was time to cut down on those extra crab cakes.)

Now everyone was racing down the hall. Unfortunately, the crab was racing a little faster and quickly closed the distance between them.

Not only did it close the distance, but it

began yelling, **"Excuse me? Ms. Finkelstein? Ms. Finkelstein, if it's not too inconvenient, may I speak with you a moment?"**

Everyone was amazed at its politeness. The fact that it could talk was kinda interesting too. Then there was the matter of its recognizing TJ even though she was in Hesper's body. (I guess giant, 15-foot crabs are sorta smart that way.) In any case, they continued down the hall, trying one locked classroom door after another, as the crab continued to

click, *click*, *click*, *click*

closer and closer.

"How does it know your name?!" Chad shouted.

"Long story," TJ shouted back.

They tried the door to Miss Grumpaton's class. It was unlocked, so they dashed inside. For a moment they were safe from the crab. Unfortunately, they were not safe from Miss Grumpaton . . . or her after-school Shakespeare Club.

With great effort the old woman (rumor is they found her fossilized footprints next to some dinosaur bones) rose from her desk and spoke:

"Behold, who hath entered my humble abode?

I knew if I wait-eth, someday one would show."

"Oh, uh, hi, Miss Grumpaton," TJ said.

"Ye must speak old-world English, when joining this club,

Those are the rules, so follow them, bub."

"Actually, we're not here for the Shakespeare Club," Chad said.

"Apparently no one else is either," Doug added as he glanced around the empty room.

Miss Grumpaton sadly sank back into her chair. For as long as she'd been teaching (the last dozen centuries or so), the club had only one member . . . her. Except for that time, long ago, when a weird writer wearing tights by the name of Billy Shakespeare showed up . . . but even he got bored and quit.

Suddenly there was a loud

scratch, scratch, scratch-ing

at the door.

"Don't answer it," TJ whispered. "Maybe he'll go away."

"Or think we're not here," Doug whispered.

Normally 15-foot crabs aren't all that bright. But this fellow was a crafty crustacean (now there's a word you can look up). He knew exactly how to discover if someone was inside. He cleared his voice and simply called, **"Knock knock."**

It was a clever trap, and Doug, who loved knock-knock jokes, felt an overwhelming need to answer.

"Don't you dare," TJ whispered.

But the crab was as persistent as he was nefarious

(oh, boy, more vocab words). He would not give up.

"Knock, knock," he repeated.

The urge to answer grew stronger.

"Hold on," Chad whispered to Doug.

"But what if it's a knock-knock joke I haven't heard?" Doug whispered.

The crab was merciless. **"Knock, knock."**

Beads of perspiration appeared on Doug's forehead.

"You can do it," Chad whispered. "You can do it."

By now Doug was starting to shake.

"You can beat this thing," TJ whispered.

But the crab was brilliant. Instead of continuing after Doug, he changed tactics. **"Knocketh, knocketh."**

Before she could stop herself, Miss Grumpaton cried out, **"Who's there-eth?"**

"Me-eth."

"Me-eth who?"

"Me-eth, the crab who hath just

SLAM-BANG

splinter, splinter, splinter

broken through-eth your classroom door-eth!"

Miss Grumpaton swooned (she was too old-school to faint), and Doug and Chad had no other choice but to leap through

CRASH-*SHATTER*

tinkle, tinkle, tinkle

the window (vowing next time to open it first).

And TJ? She would have liked to join them, but she was too busy getting cornered and preparing herself to be eaten.

"I've been waiting a long time for this," the crab said as he crawled toward her.

TJ backed up, her heart pounding in her throat.

The crab continued approaching. "A long, long time."

TJ kept backing up until she was against the wall.

The crab came closer and closer until finally the two of them were eyeball to eyeball. Then, just when TJ thought it was all over, just when she was sure she'd become a snack for this creepy crustacean (see how important it was to look up that word?), the thing suddenly rolled onto its back.

TJ gasped. "What are you doing?!"

"It's just this area, here." He clumsily pointed to his belly. "I can't seem to reach it with these ridiculous claw things. Would you mind? It really itches."

TJ stared at him with her mouth hanging open.

"Please?" He rocked a little on his back. "I'd really appreciate it."

Slowly, hesitantly, she reached out.

"I promise not to do anything stupid like eat you," he said.

At last TJ's hand touched his underbelly and she started scratching. "Like this?" she asked nervously.

"A little to the left."

"Here?"

"Ah . . . perfect."

CHAPTER SIX

Stop Being so Crabby and Shellfish . . . Just Stay Clam

(Sorry, that was too good to pass up)

TIME TRAVEL LOG:

Malibu, California, January 24—supplemental

Begin Transmission:

Subject had nice chat with our archenemy. Apparently he is still not wearing clothes (some crabs have no modesty), although his sunglasses are cool.

End Transmission

"A little higher."

TJ scratched the crab's underbelly a little higher.

"That's it . . . oh yeah." He began wiggling his claws and feet in the air. "Now if you could help me get back to my feet?"

"Pardon me?" TJ said.

"Once they're on their backs, crabs aren't so good at getting back onto their feet."

"Oh, okay." TJ grabbed his shell and started to lift.

"On three," he said as he began rocking. "One . . . two . . . three!"

Using all of her strength (and breaking only a couple of Hesper's fake fingernails), TJ successfully flipped him back onto his feet.

"I suppose you're going to eat me now, right?" she asked.

"Eat you?" The crab smiled. (Well, as much as crabs can smile.) "You're the great TJ Finkelstein. It's an honor to meet you!"

"So I'm not going to be a between-meals snack?"

"Absolutely not. If I eat you, how will you become the fantastic leader who will save our world?"

"Oh, that." TJ shook her head in disbelief. "Sounds like you've been talking to Tuna and Herby."

"Actually, everyone in our century knows about you."

"I'm sorry—what?"

"Allow me to introduce myself. I'm Bruce Bruiseabone from the 23rd century." He stuck out his claw. "It is a huge honor to meet you."

TJ hesitated, then reached out to shake his claw. "Bruce Bruisabone. They told me about you."

"They told you . . . about *me*?" He seemed embarrassed and flattered.

She nodded. "How you were naked in front of the whole world."

"Oh, that." He glanced down. TJ had never seen a crab blush, but this one was doing a pretty good imitation.

"Sorry," she said.

"That's all right," he muttered.

"I mean, I can see why you'd be mad at them and everything."

"Oh, I'm not mad," he said. "I just want to destroy them."

"Right." TJ nodded. "Just as long as you're not mad."

"I'll never forgive them for what they did."

"I hear you, but . . . ."

"But what?"

"Well, not forgiving someone, that's pretty serious stuff."

The crab cocked his head (if crabs have heads to cock). "This from the girl who won't forgive Hesper Breakahart?"

TJ looked up, startled. "Oh yeah. I'm getting there, though. You just don't know everything she's put me through."

"Oh, we know everything. Every tiny little detail about your life is recorded in our history holographs."

TJ fidgeted, wondering how tiny *tiny* was.

As if reading her mind, he answered, "*Very* tiny."

She felt no better.

He continued, "It's just too bad you're mixed up with Tuna and Herby."

TJ shrugged. "Sometimes they're not the brightest candles on the birthday cake."

"Sometimes they can't find the party."

She chuckled. "But they mean well. Their prank on you just went a little too far, that's all."

Bruce pushed up his glasses and refused to comment.

"Listen," TJ said, "is there any way you can take them back home to your century?"

"Have you seen the size of our time pods?"

TJ nodded. If his was anything like Tuna and Herby's, no way could they all fit inside. She had another thought. "They need a plutonium power pack to get their time pod up and running. Maybe you could go back to your century and bring them one?"

"Not on your life."

"Because you won't forgive them?" she asked.

"The longer they're stuck in your century, the happier I'll be."

"So you can keep coming back and bothering them," TJ said.

He shrugged (if crabs have shruggers to shrug). "Everybody needs a hobby."

Miss Grumpaton started to mumble from the floor where she had swooned.

"Uh-oh," TJ said in concern. "No offense, but I don't know if her heart can stand seeing you again."

The teacher's eyes started to flutter open.

"No problem," Bruce said. "I'll morph into something else." And just as the woman sat up and opened her eyes, Bruce pulled out his own Swiss Army knife, opened the Morphing Blade, and

krinkle . . . krackle

POOF!

turned into a 15-foot talking clam—still wearing those cool sunglasses, of course.

The old lady's eyes widened in terror.

"Hi there," he said cheerfully.

"Ohhh-eth . . . ," Miss Grumpaton cried as she swooned back to the floor.

"Must be allergic to shellfish," Bruce said.

Before TJ could answer, a voice echoed through the room. *"Bruce . . . it's time for supper."*

"Who's that?" TJ asked.

"My mom."

"Brucey . . ."

"I gotta go. It was nice meeting you."

"Uh, same here," TJ said. It wasn't exactly the truth, but she hated being rude—especially to giant clams from the 23rd century. "Oh, and about Tuna and Herby?" she asked.

"Hurry up, sweetie. It's getting cold."

"What about them?"

"Would you think about giving them a hand?"

"Brucey-woosey. . ."

Obviously embarrassed, he scrunched up his face in thought (if clams even have faces . . . if they even have thoughts). Finally he opened the Transporter Blade of his knife and answered. "No, I don't think

chugga-chugga-chugga

so . . ."

BLING!

* * *

After that enlightening conversation, it was back to the plan for

STEP THREE

Actually, this step was as easy as falling off a cliff (without having to clean up all those broken body parts). All TJ had to do was convince Principal Bustubad to let her fellow students go on a field trip to Hesper Breakahart's benefit concert.

No problem. Well, except for finding Principal Bustubad. Normally, it's easy enough. You just walk across the lawn to his office. But it's not so easy when the lawn is covered with 49½ firemen (one of them was very, very short), a squad of National Guard troops, and a dozen jet fighters

ROARRRRR-ing

overhead.

"What's happening?" TJ shouted to a passing Marine. (Oh yeah, the Marines were there too.)

"Haven't you heard?" he shouted back. "We're being invaded."

"By who?"

"Wait a minute," he shouted. "Aren't you the famous Hesper Breakahart?"

TJ gave a halfhearted nod.

"My kids love your show."

"What about the invasion?" she asked. "Who's invading us?"

"Giant crabs!" he shouted. "One attacked some reporters!"

TJ quietly groaned.

"And don't forget the clam!" a store security guard yelled. (Yeah, they were there too.) "It was spotted through a classroom window!"

TJ dropped her head into her hands. Was there no end to this madness?

"Hey, wait a minute," the guard shouted. "Aren't you Hesper Breakahart?" Before she answered, he turned to the soldiers and yelled, "Hey, everybody, it's Hesper Breakahart."

When TJ raised her head, she saw the troops gathering around her.

"Hesper Breakahart?" someone shouted. "My kids love your show!"

"Is it really her?" another yelled.

"Could I have your autograph?" someone called. "For my kids?"

"Great idea," another shouted.

"Let me grab a pen."

Before she knew it, TJ was surrounded by 49½ firemen, a National Guard squad, the Marines, one store security guard, and whoever else happened to be around to defend the country from invading seafood.

And fortunately, everyone was so starstruck that they'd completely forgotten why they were there.

NOTE TO INVADING COUNTRIES:
Start in Hollywood. No one will notice as long as they get a photo of themselves standing beside Justin Beaver.

Two hours and a whole lot of writer's cramp later, TJ managed to reach Principal Bustubad's office. He was a scary man who many believed had been a pro wrestler—and not one of the good guys. In fact, whenever students saw him approach, they made a point of taking the long way to class (often catching the #14 bus downtown, grabbing a taxi to the train station, transferring to the #2 bus, and arriving back at school sometime before sunset).

But this was all part of Tuna's elaborate plan, so TJ pressed onward. She arrived at the office just as the man was heading out the door to his car.

"Excuse me," she called. "Principal Bustubad?"

He slowed to a stop, his giant back to her.

She waited and swallowed nervously.

Then, ever so slowly and way too menacingly, he turned to face her.

TJ trembled, she shook, she broke into a good sweat . . . until he brightly chirped, "Well, hello there, Ms. Breakahart. What can I do for you today?"

She blinked, once again amazed at how being rich and famous made people think you were, well, rich and famous.

She tried to speak but, as usual, couldn't find her voice.

Mr. Bustubad waited, attempting to curl his lips into a smile. No such luck . . . though he managed a rather pleasant-looking snarl.

Well, it was now or never. TJ took a breath and began. "Mr. Bustubad, I was wondering if I could—"

"Absolutely," he interrupted.

"Absolutely?" she repeated.

"You bet. Whatever you want."

TJ blinked again. "Really?"

"Of course. You're Hesper Breakahart. My kids love your show. In fact—" he reached for a pen and notebook in his pocket—"could I have your autograph? For my little niece? She's only 22 hours old, but I'm sure she's already a fan. If not—" there was that snarl again—"I'll make sure she becomes one."

CHAPTER SEVEN

The Brilliant Plan Unfolds Not So Brilliantly

TIME TRAVEL LOG:

Long Beach, California, January 25

Begin Transmission:

Tuna's genius, which is genuinely genuine, continues in its genuinely genuine geniusness.

   TRANSLATION: *We haven't zworked it up . . . yet.*

                            End Transmission

The following morning TJ was in the limo with Tuna and Herby. It was time to begin . . .

STEP FOUR

Perform a benefit concert at the pier.

The announcement at the press conference the day before had caught everyone off guard and sent them scrambling. But that was okay. Chad had taught TJ well. If Hesper Breakahart really wanted something, all Hesper Breakahart had to do was throw a fit to get it. It was one thing for her manager, trainer, and secretary to order her around, but once she went into her Screaming Mode, she always got her way. And if she didn't get her way, her manager, trainer, and secretary would get new jobs.

But somehow, even that made TJ feel sad. If the only way Hesper could get anything was by throwing a fit and being a spoiled brat, no wonder she was always throwing fits and being a spoiled brat. The poor thing didn't know any other way to behave. And she wasn't just being a spoiled brat at work and at school. Last night when TJ went "home" to Hesper's mansion, she learned Hesper had to behave that way all the time. The moment she walked through the door, butlers and maids began waiting on her hand and foot.

"Ms. Breakahart, would you allow me to draw your bath?"

"Ms. Breakahart, would you allow me to finish your homework?"

"Ms. Breakahart, would you allow me to chew your food?"

Talk about disgusting (in more ways than one). All TJ had to do was raise her voice and people jumped to do her bidding. It was sad.

But not as sad as what would have happened to TJ's family if they had been subjected to Hesper Breakahart's super-spoiledness. That's why Herby called up Dad, pretending to be Naomi, and asked if TJ could spend the night. (Don't try this at home, kids, unless you plan to be morphed into a giant tarantula and kept in a science class cage all night . . . which is exactly what they had to do with Hesper.)

TJ gave a weary sigh. She'd definitely have some explaining to do when the boys finally fixed things and switched their bodies back. Which, according to Tuna would be . . .

"BY THE END OF THE DAY!" he shouted. Tuna wasn't being weird for shouting. It's just difficult being heard when you're floating outside the window of a limousine racing down the freeway at 65 miles an hour.

Herby, who was sitting inside the limo next to TJ, explained, "He likes the fresh air."

"JUST AS SOON AS WE OBTAIN THE

PLUTONIUM POWER PACK, WE'LL FOCUS ON REPAIRING THE THOUGHT BROADCASTER PEN!"

TJ nodded and began thinking through the final steps of the plan. They were pretty simple, really. Since Chad and Doug were students from the visiting school, no one would blame them for

—accidentally getting lost
—accidentally wandering into the restricted nuclear reactor area
—and accidentally setting off the alarms

Then, while the alarms were sounding and the guards were busy doing their guard thing—like arresting them and letting them go when they realized the boys were just dumb schoolkids—the invisible Tuna and Herby would slip past them and steal the plutonium power pack.

Tuna's plan was simple, perfect, and foolproof. TJ had nothing to worry about.

Except for the fact that it was Tuna's plan.

She turned back to him and shouted out the window, "You're sure Chad and Doug will know what to do?"

Tuna frowned and yelled, "WHAT?"

TJ repeated, "THEY'LL KNOW WHAT TO DO?"

"THEY KNOW WHAT THEY DREW?"

"NO, NO." TJ tried again. "THEY'LL KNOW WHAT TO DO?"

Tuna looked alarmed. "THEY NOW HAVE THE FLU?"

She closed her eyes and counted to a hundred. With most people you count to ten, but with these guys a hundred was the minimum daily requirement.

"Don't worry, Your Dude-ness," Herby assured her. "Everything will be stupenderous."

"You sure?" TJ asked.

"No problemo," Herby said. "Doug and Chad will be our decoys while me and Tuna take the plutonium."

TJ nodded, starting to relax.

"Your only job is to sing for the troops."

TJ started to unrelax. In fact her stomach began doing more flip-flops than a politician trying to get elected.

"What's the matter, Your Dude-ness?"

"I think we might have a problem," she said.

"Relax. Everything is perfectly gonzo."

"Except . . ."

"Except what?"

"I can't sing."

"Okay." Herby nodded.
"Okay what?"
"We have a problem."

* * *

Meanwhile, Chad, who sat in one of the school buses on the way to the concert, popped a piece of gum into his mouth and relaxed. He was sure there *wouldn't* be a problem. After all, if you can't trust 23rd-century time travelers, who can you trust? (He obviously needs to read a few more of these books.) So far, everything had gone like clockwork. The entire seventh-grade class had loaded into the school buses, which were, of course, divided into various people groups. For instance, in the back of each bus was

JOCKVILLE

where the jocks could make their usual disgusting armpit noises and toss around footballs—until, one by one, the footballs flew out the windows up in

GEEKLAND

where the geeks had opened their windows to get better reception on their geekPods, geekPads, and geekWhatevers. The section in front of them was

GOTHTOWN

where the goths were too cool to care where they sat as long as it wasn't up front in

WANNABEBURG

where Elizabeth and the rest of Hesper's posse sat so their hair wouldn't be mussed by the open windows. In front of them and isolated as far as possible was the

FORBIDDEN ISLE OF CHAPERONES

where Miss Grumpaton sat with the rest of the chaperones pretending not to notice that

    —the **goths** were giving each other piercings while
    —the **wannabes** gave each other facials while
    —the **jocks**, who'd run out of footballs, began tossing **geeks**.

Once the buses finally arrived, everyone was herded out to the pier—well, everyone but the occasional geek who was still being tossed and

SPLASH!

glug . . .

glug . . .

glug-ed . . .

into the water. (Hopefully those geekWhatevers were still under warranty.)

But the real action was with Chad and Doug. As soon as they stepped off the bus, they spotted TJ's parked limo. Good, she was already there and backstage getting ready.

"Where did *(sniff-sniff)* you say Hesper was?" Chad asked.

"Tuna and Herby said something about morphing her in TJ's room."

Chad didn't understand but nodded. "Just as long as she's not here," he said. "She couldn't stand someone else getting all the attention."

He looked over to the next pier, where the submarine was docked. It floated on the water, huge, gray, and a little scary. "Okay, there it is," he said. "Let's go."

But Doug was too busy winking and flashing his killer Chad grin at the girls who were stepping from the bus. Actually the winking and grinning wasn't as much fun as listening to them running off and giggling in excitement.

"Did you see that? Chad Steel smiled at me."

"No, he didn't. He smiled at me."

"No, he didn't. He smiled at *me*."

"C'mon, Doug," Chad said. "Knock it off."

"Sorry." Doug shrugged. Unable to resist, he gave one last wink and one last grin.

Unfortunately, it was to Miss Grumpaton, who winked and grinned back.

"Oh, brother," Chad groaned. "Let's go."

The boys strolled as casually as possible to the other pier and headed toward the submarine. The good news was all the sailors had piled out of the sub to watch and listen to Hesper Breakahart. The better news was they were too busy craning their necks to catch a glimpse of the show to care about a couple of kids wandering around.

Unfortunately, there was still some bad news . . . which we'll get to in just a second.

"Over there!" Chad motioned to a large stack of supplies in a cargo net waiting to be loaded onto the submarine.

Doug nodded. When they reached the stack, they ducked behind it and waited.

"You sure you remember where to (*sniff-sniff*) go once we're inside?" Chad asked.

"No sweat. I've got the plans Tuna gave me right here," Doug said as he reached into his back pocket. He frowned, then tried his other pocket.

Chad fidgeted and chewed his gum nervously.

Next, Doug tried his front pocket.

"Don't tell me you lost them," Chad said.

"Of course I didn't lose them," Doug answered. "I put them someplace nice and safe." He tried his other front pocket with the same lack of success.

"So safe you don't remember where?" Chad asked.

Before Doug could answer, a piece of paper suddenly appeared floating before them.

"Looking for this, dude?" Herby's voice asked as the paper started to unfold.

"You're here?" Chad whispered.

"Apparently," Tuna's voice said.

Doug quickly grabbed the paper. "Thanks."

"Are you ready?" Tuna's voice asked.

Doug nodded as Chad glanced around the stack of supplies. "Uh-(sniff-sniff)-oh."

"Uh-oh what?" Doug asked.

Chad motioned to the gangplank leading up to the submarine. Actually, it wasn't the gangplank that concerned him. It was the sailor standing guard at the bottom of the gangplank. The sailor with the very large rifle.

"What do we do?" Doug asked.

"I'm thinking," Tuna's voice said. "I'm thinking."

Somehow Chad didn't find that comforting.

And then it happened—the bad news I warned you about.

"Ladies and gentlemen-en-en." An announcer's voice echoed across the water. "It is my pleasure to introduce to you-ou-ou the star of her own TV series and a legend in her own mind—er, time-ime-ime . . ."

"Sounds like he really knows her," Doug chuckled.

"Please give a warm round of applause to Ms. Hesper-er-er . . . Breakahart-art-art!"

Actually, even that wasn't the bad news. The bad news was when TJ started to sing. Fortunately that won't be till the next chapter, so you have plenty of time to prepare yourself.

CHAPTER EIGHT

The Plan Continues
to ~~Unfold~~ Unravel

TIME TRAVEL LOG:

Long Beach, California, January 25-supplemental

Begin Transmission:

Tuna's plan works brilliantly. Well, except for possibly destroying the entire state of California. Not a huge loss, but I will miss the surfing (and all those goofy celebrities doing goofy things). Oh, well; you win a few, you destroy a few.

End Transmission

Backstage, TJ heard the music begin to play.

"Ms. Breakahart!" the stagehand shouted over the music while handing her a water bottle. "You're on!"

TJ nodded and looked about desperately. "Tuna!" she whispered. "Herby!"

But Tuna and Herby were nowhere to be found. They'd left her side as soon as they saw the buses arrive.

"Ms. Breakahart!" The stagehand pulled back the curtain. "They're waiting!"

TJ nodded and smiled. Then she smiled and nodded.

Out in the audience, she could hear them starting to chant:

"Hesper . . . Hesper . . . Hesper . . ."

She took a sip from the water bottle for courage. Then another sip. Then another—

"MS. BREAKAHART!"

Well, it was now or never (though the never part sounded a lot more appealing). After another sip and a few more nods and smiles thrown in for good measure, TJ stepped through the curtains.

And the crowd went wild.

The **SAILORS** took pictures for their wives and kids back home.

The **WANNABES** waved and blew kisses.
The **GOTHS** tried their best to look bored.
The **CHAPERONES** still tried to stop
the **JOCKS** from tossing
the

SPLASH!

    glug . . .

        glug . . .

            glug. . .

                GEEKS into the water.

Yes, sir, it was quite a show.

Then there was the one onstage. TJ was definitely going through her own drama. She'd had no idea how scary it would be having a thousand people staring at her. She had no idea that her body would start to freeze up, making it harder and harder to walk.

Move your left foot forward! she thought. *Good. Now your right foot. Come on, you can do it. Good. Now your left.* (It's always a smart idea to go back to the basics when you're scared spitless—or in TJ's case, walkless.)

Eventually she made it to center stage. Terrific! Fantastic! She'd done it!

Well, not exactly. There was still the minor problem of having to sing. She grinned and nodded. She took a sip from her water bottle.

"HESPER . . . HESPER . . . HESPER"

She nodded and grinned. She took another sip. (At least she was good at something.)

"HESPER . . . HESPER . . . HESPER"

Finally she scrunched her eyes tight, opened her mouth wide, and tried something she wasn't so good at. She'd been hoping that with Hesper's fantastically great looks, she might somehow have Hesper's fantastically great voice. Unfortunately, she was fantastically wrong. The best way to sum up her performance was

Please circle appropriate letter
A: Awful
B: Hideous

C: Okay for the sound track of a horror movie

D: Okay if that sound track is only of screaming people being tortured

E: All of the above

If you selected *E*, you must have been there. (And I hope you've gone to see a doctor to have your hearing restored.)

I don't want to be mean, but do you remember those howling dogs across the street from the school's choir room? Well, now you can add three wailing cats, two writhing rats, and a partridge fainting from a pear tree. Oh, and an entire pod of whales that suddenly turned fin and swam away, hoping to be caught by whalers so they'd be put out of their misery.

And that was just TJ's first note.

* * *

"There's our cue!" Tuna shouted as he winced, cringed, and fought back the urge to jump into the water and join those whales. "Go, go, go!"

Chad and Doug went, went, went!

Fortunately, the guard at the gangplank was too busy covering his ears and kicking away crazed cats and rats (not to mention dodging a falling partridge) to notice the boys and their invisible companions slipping past him.

Within seconds all four were inside the sub. They quickly wound their way through the passageways, this way and that, that way and this. Of course it would have been a lot easier if they hadn't asked Herby for help.

"Is this the right turn?" Doug asked.

"No, left," Herby said.

"Left?" Doug asked.

"Right."

"You mean, turn right here."

"No, I mean turn left here."

"Left?"

"Right. Turn left."

(See what I mean?)

"Left?" Doug asked.

"Right," Herby agreed.

But with no sailors to stop them, they eventually arrived at the door Tuna insisted led to the nuclear reactor. And if you don't trust Tuna, there was one other clue—the sign above the door that read

NUCLEAR REACTOR—
POSSIBLE RADIATON (WE MEAN A LOT)

AUTHORIZED PERSONNEL ONLY!
(which we're pretty sure you're not)

It was a wordy sign, but the boys got the message. Without hesitation (but with a whole lot of prayers) they entered the brightly lit room. It had hundreds of buttons, switches, and gauges . . . which had hundreds of even wordier signs.

WARNING:

PRESS THIS BUTTON ONLY IF YOU WANT TO GLOW IN THE DARK LIKE A NIGHT-LIGHT FOR 2.3 MILLION YEARS.

WARNING:

FLIP THIS SWITCH ONLY IF YOU'VE PAID UP YOUR LIFE INSURANCE AND AREN'T ALLERGIC TO DYING.

WARNING:

AFTER TURNING THIS DIAL,
IMMEDIATELY RUN FOR COVER,
THOUGH IT WON'T DO YOU
(OR THE WORLD) ANY GOOD.

BEST OF LUCK ANYWAY.

The good news was no one felt like pressing any buttons or dialing any dials.

The better news was the intruder alarm began to

BLEEP . . . BLEEp . . . BLEEP

exactly as they hoped. Chad and Doug had created a commotion, which made them the decoys. Now as whatever sailors were left on board ran after them, Tuna and Herby could grab the plutonium power pack completely unnoticed.

Everything was going according to plan. Unfortunately, it was still Tuna's plan, which meant a few surprises like . . .

Wooozazazazazazazazazaza . . .

"What's that?" Chad said.

Tuna answered, "It sounds like an electromagnetic alarm oscillating at the precise frequency to neutralize any and all electronic devices."

"Right," Chad said. "And if you were speaking like a human being, that would mean . . ."

He got his answer by the sound coming from Herby's pocket. A sound that did not bring back fond memories.

TINKA . . .

DOINK-DOINK-DOINK

"What's that?" Doug asked.

"Our Acme Thought Broadcaster Pen," Tuna said as Herby reached into his pocket. "The electromagnetic wave must have set it off."

"So why is it getting

DOINK-DOINK-DOINK

louder?" Chad asked.

Tuna looked at Herby.

Herby looked at Tuna.

DOINK-DOINK-DOINK

"Guys?" Chad repeated.

"Actually the reason is quite simple," Tuna said.

"Which is?" Doug asked.

"Because it's going to blow us to

DOINK-DOINK-DOINK

SMITHEREENS!" Herby screamed.

"WHAT DO WE DO?!" Chad yelled.

"TAKE IT AND GET IT OFF THE SUBMARINE!" Tuna shouted. "GET IT AWAY FROM THE PLUTONIUM OR WE'LL HAVE A MAJOR CATASTROPHE!"

Now to be honest, Chad had never thought much about being a hero. Nor was he particularly fond of grabbing noisy Thought Broadcaster Pens. But both seemed like pretty good ideas compared to standing around and being blown away with the rest of California.

But first there was the little problem of the guard who appeared around the corner. "What are you doing?!" he shouted. "Stay right there! YOU'RE UNDER ARREST!"

Chad would have loved to obey . . . if it wasn't for his habit of wanting to live. So he grabbed the pen from Herby and shouted to Doug, "RUN!"

Doug didn't have to be told twice. (Actually, he didn't have to be told once because he was already hightailing it out of there.)

The guard took off after them. "STOP RIGHT THERE!" he shouted. "STOP RUNNING!"

But Chad and Doug didn't stop running, nor did the pen stop

DOINK-DOINK-DOINK-ing

They raced down the corridors as fast as they could, retracing their steps, taking lefts when they had taken rights and rights when they had taken lefts

. . . or was it rights when they'd taken lefts and lefts when they had—

Forget it. The important thing was the guard kept getting closer.

And the pen kept getting

DOINK-DOINK-DOINK

louder.

At last they reached the submarine's exit and ran down the gangplank.

"WHAT DO WE DO WITH IT?!" Chad yelled over the noise.

"THROW IT AWAY!" Doug shouted. "THROW IT AS FAR AS YOU CAN!"

Being the excellent athlete, Chad leaned back to throw the pen as far from them as possible. And he might have succeeded if he wasn't still in Doug's body. But there is no cure for geekiness . . . which explains why, instead of a beautiful forward pass, his hand accidentally hit his head, which meant he accidentally dropped the pen, which meant it accidentally fell to the—

clatter

roll . . . roll . . . roll . . .

pier.

The good news was all that *DOINK*-ing suddenly stopped.

"That was close," Chad said, chomping away on his gum.

"I'll say," Doug agreed.

The bad news was the pen burst into a rather bright and annoying

FLASH

CHAPTER NINE

The Plan Succeeds Magnificently

(except for the part where it fails miserably)

TIME TRAVEL LOG:

Long Beach, California, January 25—supplemental

Begin Transmission:

Everything is going according to plan. Well, not our plan, but somebody's . . . I hope.

End Transmission

The good news—as in fantastic, wonderful, fall-to-your-knees-in-thanks kinda news—was that the FLASH was so bright TJ quit singing and opened her eyes.

The bad news was . . . everything else.

Well, not everything—just the screaming panic that swept through the crowd when everyone in the audience who had seen the FLASH switched places with everyone else.

Yeah, I'm afraid so.

The **jocks** switched with the **geeks** . . .
"Hey, who stole my muscles?!"

The **geeks** switched with the **jocks** . . .
"Hey, who stole my brains?!"

The **goths** switched with the **wannabes** . . .
"Hey, who stole my tongue studs?!"

The **wannabes** switched with the **goths** . . .
"Ow, wath wong with ma tongue?!"

But the scariest switch of all was Elizabeth Mindlessfan trading places with Miss Grumpaton. (Tough to say who got the worst of that deal.)

"AUGH!" Elizabeth screamed, hiding her wrinkled face.

"Hubba-hubba!" Miss Grumpaton said, checking out her brand-new bod.

Everything and everybody had turned crazy. And TJ knew exactly who to blame. "TUNA!!!" she cried. "HERBY!!!"

But Tuna and Herby had their own set of problems.

* * *

The compartment holding the plutonium power packs was not hard to find, thanks to Tuna's years of training and his careful research. Then there was the sign above it, which didn't hurt either.

WARNING:

PLUTONIUM PACKS ARE HERE . . .
UNLESS YOU'RE A SPY OR BAD GUY
WHO WANTS TO STEAL THEM, IN WHICH
CASE THEY'RE FOUR BLOCKS DOWN THE
STREET, LEFT AT THE 7-ELEVEN, AND IN
THE BACK DUMPSTER. KNOCK TWICE
AND ASK FOR JOE. OR CALL THE POLICE
DEPARTMENT, WHO WILL BE MORE
THAN WILLING TO HELP YOU.

(And you thought those signs in the last chapter were ridiculous.)

After carefully putting on protective suits (invisible, of course), Tuna removed the small, square plutonium pack and put it in his pocket while Herby scribbled out a quick note saying they were just borrowing the pack and would return it in the next century . . . or two.

So far, so good.

Next they wound their way back through the sub's passageways to the exit.

So far-er, so good-er.

What wasn't so good was when they stepped out onto the pier. They found plenty of confusion since even the sailors had traded places with each other (although they all looked the same in those uniforms, so it didn't make much difference—except maybe to the sailors). But the real problem came when a 30-foot waterspout suddenly appeared and moved toward the pier.

"Well, now," Herby said, "there's something you don't see every day."

"Actually," Tuna calmly replied as he turned his back on the spout to enlighten Herby, "waterspouts form all the time. They're like miniature tornadoes created by the wind."

"Except . . ." Herby nervously looked past Tuna.

"Except what?"

"How many waterspouts leap off the water and onto the pier?"

"The odds of that are extremely rare," Tuna said.

Herby continued to stare past Tuna, his eyes growing wide. "And what are the odds of that same waterspout racing toward two 23rd-century time travelers and coming to a stop directly behind them?"

Tuna frowned, whipped out his calculator, and did the math. "That would be . . . let's see now, add the 2, carry the 3, divide by $3,569,896,042^{1/3}$ and we get . . . right, exactly as I thought."

"What?" Herby asked.

"The odds are absolutely impossible."

Herby smiled weakly and pointed above Tuna's head. "You might want to tell that to the giant waterspout behind you."

Tuna spun around just as the waterspout spoke.

"Hello, boys."

Tuna glanced down at his calculator, then tossed it into the ocean.

"You really didn't think you could get away from me, did you?"

"Bruce?" Tuna ventured. "Bruce Bruiseabone, is that really you?"

"That's right," the waterspout said, pushing up his very cool sunglasses. **"Pretty neat disguise, huh?"**

Herby shrugged. "Better than the crab."

"So, uh . . ." Tuna cleared his throat while sneaking looks around for an escape. "Is this the part where you're going to torture, torment, and destroy us?"

"Nah," the waterspout said. **"Don't need to."**

"Why not?"

"See all those sailors standing around staring at us?"

"Staring at *you*," Tuna corrected. "Because, as I previously mentioned, the odds of a talking waterspout are—"

"Please, let's not go through that again."

"But they can't see us, dude," Herby explained. "We're, like, totally invisible."

"You WERE totally invisible," the waterspout corrected.

"Were?" Tuna asked.

"Until I collapse and dump all my water on top of you."

And to prove he wasn't lying (waterspouts have to keep up their reputations for honesty), he leaned forward and

SPLASh!

drip . . .

drip . . .

drip-ed . . .

all over them.

"Oh, man," Herby groaned, "look at my clothes. They're soaked."

Unfortunately, the water on Herby's clothes wasn't the only thing people could see.

"Hey, Bob, look at them two semivisible fellers!" a sailor shouted.

"I'm Bill, Ben," the other answered.

"I'm Burt, Bill," the first replied. "Look like ghosts, don't they, Bud!"

"I'm Barney, Burt."

"Well, whoever we are," Bill shouted, "I'm betting they aren't ghosts, but spies!"

And despite their major identity crises, one very confused and very angry group of sailors (with some very large and very angry rifles) started after Tuna and Herby.

Being the brains of the operation, Tuna brought out the tried-and-true solution they always used.

"Herby?"

"Yes, Tuna."

"I have a tried-and-true solution."

"What's that, Tuna?"

"RUN!!!!"

And run they did, very quickly. With lots of

drip . . . drip . . .

drip . . . drip . . . drip-ing

"Which way?" Herby shouted.

"Into the audience!" Tuna yelled.

For once it was a pretty good idea. (Accidents happen.) Everyone in the audience was too freaked about their new bodies to notice little things like soggy time travelers, charging sailors, or a yelling waterspout with sunglasses. (That's right: ol' Bruce had pulled himself together from whatever water was left on the pier and was racing after them too.)

"You're not getting away this time!" he shouted.

Maybe they were, maybe they weren't. The point is, it didn't stop them from trying. Tuna and Herby ran through the crowd as fast as they could

duck . . . *dodge* . . . and *sidestep*

the **jocks** who were now being

fling . . . *flung* . . . *flang-ed*

by the **geeks** who were

SPLASh!

glug . . .

glug . . .

glug-ing . . .

them into the ocean as the **wannabes** were

unbolting . . . unriveting . . . and unscrewing . . .

their piercings, while the **goths** were desperately looking for dirty motor oil to

smear . . . slime . . . and goop . . .

into their hair.

Of course, Chad and Doug had also joined the crowd, which explains why Miss Grumpaton began chasing Doug. "Oh, Chad, sweetie," she shouted. "Remember me? The girl you winked at when I stepped off the bus!"

Yes, sir, things couldn't get more confusing . . . or gross.

"Duck behind the stage!" Tuna shouted to Herby. "They'll never think of looking for us there!"

It was another swell idea . . . except for being totally wrong.

"They're running behind the stage!" the sailors shouted. "We'll circle around and cut them off!" And being true to their word (sailors are as concerned about their reputations as waterspouts), they rounded the corner behind the stage and spotted our heroes. "Stop right there!" they shouted.

Tuna and Herby came to a stop. There's something about dozens of angry sailors blocking your path that will do that to a person. Especially if they're holding a dozen angry rifles. But the guys weren't ready to give up. Not yet.

"Back up," Tuna whispered. "Turn around and make a run for it."

Another swell idea except for . . .

"Well, hi there." Bruce appeared behind them, blocking their exit.

"Uh-oh," Herby whispered. "We're zworked."

"You can say that again," Tuna agreed.

"Uh-oh. We're—"

"Herb?"

"Yes, Tuna?"

"Put a sock in it."

Herby nodded as they watched the sailors close in from the front . . .

"Be careful, Jim," one of the sailors whispered. "They're a tricky pair."

"Actually, I'm Jerry, Joe."
"Actually, I'm Jed, Jerry."

. . . while Bruce closed in from behind.

"So what will it be, guys? A nice drowning here at the pier? Or should I pick you up, spin you out to sea, and let you sink there?"

"That's an excellent question," Tuna said.

"Thanks. I try."

"Can we think it over and get back to you tomorrow?"

"Hmmm . . . no."

CHAPTER TEN

Showdown

"And just what are you doing!?"

Everyone turned to see TJ (aka Hesper Breakahart) standing behind Bruce (aka the waterspout) with her hands on her hips (aka her hips). She was doing her best to pretend she was angry. Of course she knew everyone would think it was weird talking to a waterspout (especially one wearing sunglasses) but she had worked out her own plan. One that might actually work. It was a risky plan, but if everyone in the 23rd century thought she was going to be somebody special, then maybe she would act like . . . well, somebody special.

"Oh, hi, Ms. Finkelstein," the waterspout said. **"How are you today?"**

TJ disguised her fear by continuing to act angry. "Don't 'how are you' me, Bruce Bruiseabone."

"Is there a problem?"

She crossed her arms. "You tell me. Are you picking on Tuna and Herby again?"

"No, ma'am."

She tapped her foot. "Bruce . . ."

"Well . . ." The waterspout's voice cracked (well, as much as any waterspout's voice can crack). **"Maybe a little."**

"Even after our talk about forgiveness?"

"I told you I can't forgive them after what they did to me."

"And I told you it was an accident." TJ pointed to the boys. "Just look at them. I mean, can anything be sadder than these bungling goofballs?"

"That's no excuse," Bruce said. **"Just because they're ignorant goofballs doesn't—"**

"Hey," Tuna corrected, "she said *bungling* goofballs, not ignorant ones."

"Sorry," Bruce replied. **"Just because they're bungling goofballs doesn't mean I should forgive them."**

Now it's true, before the last 48 hours, TJ would have agreed. But then she'd switched places with Hesper. Until that switch she figured no one had the right to be a jerk. And maybe they didn't. But after you've walked a mile (or a couple days) in someone else's shoes and understand the hard stuff they're going through, you at least start to understand why they act that way. And if you understand, it makes it easier to forgive.

It made a lot of sense. And with that thought came another.

Taking a breath for courage, TJ stepped past the waterspout. "Excuse me," she said as she joined Tuna and Herby. "Can I borrow that Thought Broadcaster thingy?"

"Absolutely," Herby said. "Except . . ."

"Except what?"

"We don't have it."

"But *we* do," Chad called from behind the sailors. He raised the pen above their heads so she could see.

For a brief second the shy and frightened TJ tried to resurface. Who was she to talk in front of everybody—especially those angry sailors with their angry rifles? Who was she to take matters into her own hands and suggest a solution? She was a nobody. Just some stupid kid. But there was another part of TJ, the part that believed what the time travelers had been saying about her—that someday she would be a strong and brave leader. And if that was true . . . couldn't she try to be a little bit of that person right now? If that was true, couldn't she move a little bit into her future today?

With another breath, she called out to Chad, "Can I see it?"

"Sure." Chad moved past the sailors and handed her the pen.

"Wh-what-what are you doing?" Bruce asked, nervously eyeing the pen.

"If you don't think you should forgive them," TJ said, "then maybe you should trade places with them. You know, just to see how hard it is being them."

"You can't do that," Bruce said. He turned to Tuna and Herby. **"Tell her she can't do that."**

"We'd like to," Tuna said, "except . . ."

"Except what?"

"She's the great TJ Finkelstein."

"Besides—" Herby lowered his voice, embarrassed— "for some reason, she doesn't always trust us."

"Well, I'll . . . I'll just close my eyes," Bruce said. **"She can't transfer me if my eyelids are closed."**

"A gonzo idea, except . . ."

"Except what?"

"Waterspouts don't have eyelids."

TJ reached for the pen's clicker. "So what do you say, Bruce? You want to trade places with one of these guys?"

Herby raised his hand and began to cry, "Oh, me, me. Pick me, dude. Pick me!"

"Or do you want to forgive them?" TJ's heart pounded so hard she was afraid he could hear it. But she wouldn't back down. If she was the great

TJ Finkelstein, then she would act like the great TJ Finkelstein.

Bruce swallowed—not as easy as you might think for a waterspout.

TJ waited as Herby continued waving his hand and calling out, "Me, me, me! Pick me; pick me!"

At last Bruce pushed up his sunglasses and said,

"Well . . . all right. I'll let them go."

Herby sighed. "Bummer."

"But just this once." And before anyone could react, Bruce pulled out his own Swiss Army knife (sold at 23rd-century time-travel stores everywhere).

"Hey, Wilbur," one of the sailors said. "There's something else you don't see every day."

"I'm Wendell, Willy."

"I'm Warren, Wendell."

As they spoke, Bruce opened a blade and

BLING!

the waterspout disappeared without a trace . . . well, except for a couple of confused halibut who had been in the water and were left flapping around on the pier.

"All right!" Tuna shouted.

"You did it!" Doug cried, giving TJ a high five. "Way to go!"

"Nice work," Chad agreed.

TJ looked on, as surprised as they were. But it was true: she had succeeded.

"We're home free!" Herby yelled.

"Not exactly," Tuna said.

"What do you mean?"

Tuna nodded toward the angry sailors still holding those angry rifles.

"No problemo," Herby said as he pulled out his own knife.

"Hey, look," one of the sailors shouted, "there's another one of them Swiss Army knives."

"Actually, ours is the super deluxe model," Tuna said. "It is far more costly."

"And expensive," Herby said, pulling open the blade, which started to

chugga-chugga-chugga

Another sailor commented, "It doesn't sound the same, does it, Trent?"

"Actually, I'm Tommy, Troy."

"Actually, I'm Tyler, Tom."

BLING!

* * *

The good news was TJ, Chad, and Doug disappeared from the pier.

The bad news was they were still with Tuna and Herby.

The worse news was they appeared to be inside somebody's

ZAP . . . ZAP . . . ZAP . . .

Zombie Vampires with Laser Guns computer game.

And the worst news was that they were in level 16 of the game, where the zombie vampires never

ZAP . . . BLAM

"Ouch!"

ZAP . . . BLAM

"Yikes!"

ZAP . . . BLAM

"That really smarts!"

miss.

"HERBY!" TJ shouted.

"Sorry, Your Dude-ness," Herby said as he reentered the coordinates and

chugga-chugga-chugga

BLING!-ed

them into some very cramped and very dark darkness.

"Mow whar r whee?" Chad asked. (Which should have been *"Now where are we,"* except it's hard talking when someone's elbow is in your mouth.)

"Mi mon't know," TJ answered. (It's just as hard when someone's knee is there.) "Bwat it shoore izz cwamped and daawrk."

They didn't have to wait long to find out.
Unfortunately, what they found out was

BLAM!

"WE'VE BEEN SHOT FROM A CANNON!"

Doug yelled. (Which is just the sort of thing you
would yell when you've been transported into a
circus act that fires cannons.)

Anyway, they all

land   *land*

land

land   *land-ed*

in a giant net. And Herby, who would not be put
off by a few broken bones, pulled out the knife
again and

chugga-chugga-chugga

BLING!

finally landed them in—

"At last," TJ sighed with relief, "we're in my
bedroom."

"Of course we are," Herby said. "Where did you
expect?"

Tuna turned to Chad and explained, "He likes to
take the scenic route."

"Looky!" Herby shouted as he proudly pulled the
plutonium pack from his pocket.

"We did it!" Tuna cried. "Now all we need is that
chili recipe and some African ostriches and we'll have
enough fuel to return home!"

Herby nodded in enthusiasm. "I can practically smell
my mom's home-cooked bean right now." (Apparently
they're a little short on food in the 23rd century.)

"Guys?" TJ asked.

Tuna agreed, "I can't wait to crawl into my very

own shoe box and get some real sleep." (Apparently they're a little short on space, too.)

"Guys?" TJ shouted. They turned to her as she motioned to Chad and Doug. "What about them?"

"I'm afraid they'll have to stay here," Tuna said.

"Unless they bring their own bean," Herby added.

TJ shook her head. "No, I mean you've still got everybody all switched around. What are you going to do to fix that?"

"Oh yeah," Tuna said, scrunching his head into a frown.

"Oh yeah," Herby said, imitating his friend and his frown.

After a long moment, Tuna turned back to TJ and asked, "I don't suppose people would get used to the slight changes in their lives?"

TJ blew Hesper's hair out of her face and gave him a look.

"No," Tuna sighed, "I suppose not." He turned to Herby. "So, what do you think, Herb?"

"You know, that's really not my specialty, Tuna."

"Switching people back?"

"Thinking."

"I see your point."

"I thought you might."

"Hmm . . . ," Tuna said.

"Hmm . . . ," Herby repeated.

"Come on, guys," TJ complained. "You just can't leave us this way."

"Are you sure?" Doug asked, checking out his cool Chad-body. "Some of us might get used to the sacrifice."

TJ turned to Tuna. "What about fixing that pen thingy?"

"As you may recall, it is the Thought Broadcaster Pen that got us into this predicament in the first place."

"Then what about your other gizmos?" TJ asked. "What about the Morphing Blade?"

"Actually," Tuna replied, "we tried it on Hesper before we left for the pier this morning."

"What happened?" TJ asked.

Herby cleared his throat. "It's kinda, like, stuck on the GOLDFISH setting."

"The what?!"

He nodded toward TJ's fishbowl. George, her goldfish, had a new companion that he was chasing around inside it.

TJ's eyes widened. "That's . . . that's terrible."

"Not for George," Herby said.

"I think he's in love," Tuna agreed.

Everyone watched as George continued chasing Hesper around and around.

"Good thing Chad's not the jealous type," Doug said.

"What about the Reverse Beam Blade?" TJ asked. "Remember, you used it on Elizabeth when she broke into my house?"

"You wish for us to reverse time so none of this happened?" Tuna asked.

TJ nodded. "Isn't that what you did with those pirate ships? And when those *Treasure Island* characters came to life?"

"Wait a minute," Chad said, "that stuff really happened?" He snapped his gum nervously. "I thought it was just a dream."

TJ shrugged. "I'm afraid it did."

"Wow . . . ," Chad said. "The way you tried to save your sister then—you were fantastic."

TJ fidgeted under the compliment.

"Actually, Your Dude-ness," Herby said as he reached back into his pocket for the knife, "you might have a point."

"Wait, wait!" Doug said. "You're going to run everything backwards to *before* we were switched?"

"Exactamento, dude."

"So Chad and me—" Doug checked out his super Chadness, then looked over to Chad and his geeky Dougness—"we'll be back in our own bodies."

"That's right."

Doug gave a heavy sigh.

"And like before, we're not going to remember any of this?" Chad asked.

TJ nodded. "You won't, but apparently I will. Lucky me."

Instead of answering, Chad looked directly into TJ's eyes. And even though it was Doug's body and Doug's eyes, TJ still felt her knees get just a little weak. She glanced away, but when she looked back, he was still staring.

"What are you doing?" Doug asked.

Chad quit chewing his gum and answered, "I'm just trying to remember as much as I can."

TJ felt her face growing hot.

To make matters worse, he added, "There's a lot more to you than I would have guessed."

She shifted under his gaze.

He continued, nodding toward Tuna and Herby, "How you stood up to everyone for your friends . . . how you stayed calm and figured stuff out when everyone else was going crazy . . . I can see what they mean."

"About what?" TJ croaked.

"About you becoming a great leader."

TJ tried swallowing but her swallower seemed to be broken.

More softly, he added, "Even if I won't remember
. . . I'm glad I got to know the real TJ Finkelstein."

This time she did not look away. She doubted she
could.

"All right," Herby called as he prepared to open
the blade of his knife. "Everybody ready?"

Chad gave TJ a smile and answered, "Ready."

"Can't I just keep his hair?" Doug asked.

"Sorry, dude."

Doug gave another sigh and nodded. "All right."

"Okay," Herby said. "It's been real. We'll see all
you dudes and dude-nesses . . . earlier." He opened
the blade and

Raaaapha . . .
Reeeepha . . . Riiiipha . . .

BOING-oing-oing-oing-oing!

everything started going . . .

".reilrae . . . sessen-edud dna sedud uoy lla ees
ll'eW .lear neeb s'tI" .dias ybreH ",yakO"

".thgir llA" .deddon dna hgis rehtona evag guoD

backward.

CHAPTER ELEVEN

Mopping Up

TIME TRAVEL LOG:

Malibu, California, January 23 . . . again

Begin Transmission:
Just like old times . . . except for being entirely
different.

End Transmission

Suddenly TJ was back in the choir room auditioning
for the solo for the spring concert. Once again eyes
watered, dogs howled, and choir directors threw
up. Of course TJ would have preferred Herby to
reverse time just a little further back so she didn't
have to go through all that embarrassment again.

But considering Herby's awful aim, she felt lucky not to be back in preschool . . . or inside her mom's tummy waiting to be born.

"Well, now," Mr. Hatemijob was saying, "your singing is so . . . how can I put it? . . . the worst thing I've ever heard in my entire life!"

TJ winced but remembered there would be more to come.

"Maybe you should transfer from my class and attend another that would put your unique vocal skills to better use."

"Yeah—" Hesper Breakahart giggled from across the room—"like sign language."

And since Hesper giggled, Elizabeth Mindlessfan and the rest of Hesper's wannabes giggled.

Yes, sir, nothing beats the good ol' days. Next would come Chad's comment. And right on cue, he spoke up:

"I don't know," he said. "TJ wasn't *that* bad."

WAIT A MINUTE! TJ thought. *Did he say my name? That's not how it happened the first time!* She shook her head, wondering if she'd heard right. *Does he actually know my name?* She threw a surprised look at Chad and saw him smiling . . . at *her*. And not just his polite smile. This was the very same one he'd given her just before they were transported back in time.

She leaned over to Tuna, who was floating beside her. "Did you hear that?" she whispered.

Tuna nodded.

"Does he . . . do you think he remembers?"

"If he was chewing gum, he may remember bits and pieces."

"What do you mean?" TJ whispered.

"The chemical composition of chewing gum can create adverse effects in regards to the penetrating power of—"

TJ held up her hand. "English, please?"

Tuna cleared his throat and tried again. "The rays don't work so great around gum."

"That's how we were able to keep the plutonium pack," Herby said. "By wrapping it in bubble gum."

"You've still got the plutonium power pack?" TJ asked.

Tuna nodded and beamed. "One step closer to home."

That was good news. Unfortunately, there was some bad. TJ wasn't the only one who noticed Chad's special smile to her. So did Hesper Breakahart.

"You're right." Hesper smiled sweetly at TJ while giving her dagger looks. "She's not bad; she's worse than bad." The wannabes giggled, but she wasn't finished. "In fact, someone needs to invent a word to describe it."

More laughter as Elizabeth Mindlessfan added, "But then it would be so nasty, we couldn't say it in public."

TJ's face was growing hot in anger. How dare Hesper talk about her like that? How dare she be so rude and mean and . . .

But even as TJ thought this, other memories came to the surface. Memories of a manager who pushed Hesper every second of every day. Memories of exhausting work under impossible conditions . . . of having to watch every single bite of food she ate . . . of not being able to trust anyone to tell her the truth . . . of being so busy she couldn't even spend time with her own mother.

And as these memories surfaced and TJ remembered how hard those two days had been, her heart softened. She no longer saw the spoiled, mean-spirited TV star. Instead, she saw the tired, frightened little girl everybody used for their advantage.

And as TJ saw this, forgiveness flooded in. Before she knew it, she was smiling back at Hesper. "Yeah," she laughed, "I really am pretty bad, aren't I."

"Worse than bad," Hesper said.

TJ nodded and smiled. "You're probably right."

"I know I'm right. Just ask anybody who isn't completely deaf."

It was hard to keep smiling, but TJ had made up her mind to forgive Hesper, no matter what she said or did. Turning to the choir director, TJ asked, "Mr. Hatemijob, why don't you let Hesper sing the solo? I mean, she's got the perfect voice."

The choir director frowned. "I don't know. That would mean she'd have five solos in one concert."

"I could handle it, Mr. Hatemijob," Hesper said. "You know how great I am. In fact, we could change the name from the spring concert to the Hesper Breakahart Concert. It really has a much better ring to it, wouldn't you agree?"

"Oooh, what a great idea," Elizabeth squealed.

"Oooh, what a great idea," the wannabes agreed.

Before Mr. Hatemijob could answer, the bell rang and everyone headed to the back of the room to gather their books. "I'll let you know," he called over the noise, though it was doubtful anyone heard.

TJ joined the others to get her backpack. It felt odd, being nice to Hesper like that—especially when Hesper didn't return the favor. Then again, maybe Hesper wanted to be nice and just didn't know how.

"Get out of my way, loser," Hesper said, brushing past her.

Or not.

TJ had just hoisted her backpack onto her shoulders when she heard Chad say, "That was pretty cool."

She turned to see his killer grin and sparkling blue eyes pointing directly at her.

"The way you treated Hesper a minute ago," he said. "Very cool."

TJ smiled, pleased and embarrassed.

"Oh, Chad, sweetie?"

They turned to see Hesper standing in the doorway. "Are you going to walk me to class or not?"

"I'll catch up with you in a sec," he said.

"Well, hurry. You know how heavy these books can be," she whined.

"I'll be right there," he said.

As Hesper headed out the door, Chad turned back to TJ. "Listen, I don't want to weird you out or anything, but I had this crazy dream about you last night."

"Me?" TJ croaked.

"Yeah, and it got me to thinking. I mean, here we are neighbors and everything, and I barely know you."

TJ shrugged as they started for the door. "You've been busy."

"Yeah, but still . . ." He cleared his throat. "Maybe

we could, you know, grab a coffee or a soda after school sometime and just talk."

TJ wanted to agree, but first she had to remember how to breathe. From the corner of her eye, she saw Herby lifting the stack of sheet music by the window. And since Hesper was already gone (and Herby was the jealous type) she knew exactly who the new target would be.

"Stop it," she whispered.

"I'm sorry?" Chad asked.

The stack floated across the room toward them.

TJ frowned hard at Herby and whispered, "Don't you dare."

Chad looked puzzled. "I'm sorry. I wasn't trying to be rude."

"No, no," TJ said, "not you." She watched with relief as Herby slowly came to a stop. "That's better," she said. "And don't try it again."

Chad watched her, more confused than ever.

Feeling his eyes on her but not wanting to explain, she turned and continued toward the door. "Coffee, you said?"

Chad followed. "Yeah. Or a burger or something. If it's cool with you. You know, just to talk."

Somehow, someway, TJ managed to answer. "Yeah, I think I'd like that."

Her voice was hoarse and she was a little too loud. But it was the only way she could hear herself speak over the pounding of her heart.

"I'd like that a lot."

RED ROCK MYSTERIES

BRYCE AND ASHLEY TIMBERLINE are normal 13-year-old twins, except for one thing—they discover action-packed mystery wherever they go. Wanting to get to the bottom of any mystery, these twins find themselves on a nonstop search for truth.

CP0140

Would you like Bill Myers

(author of TJ and the Time Stumblers series)

to visit your school?

Send him an e-mail:

Bill@billmyers.com

Visit tyndale.com/tjandthetimestumblers